THE LIGHTS IN THE SKY ARE STARS

The Lights in the Sky are Stars

by

FREDRIC BROWN

E. P. DUTTON & COMPANY, INC.

NEW YORK

Contents

Section: 1997   PAGE: 9

1998   45

1999   99

2000   201

2001   219

1997

1997

I'D BEEN intending to stay a few more days but, that afternoon, something changed my mind. It was the sight of myself in the mirror in my brother Bill's bathroom. Stark naked, dripping wet, standing on one leg because I have only one leg to stand on, water running noisily out of the tub behind me, I decided to leave that very night.

Time was running out of me like the water out of that bathtub. The sight of myself in the long mirror on the door showed me that, all too clearly.

A mirror doesn't lie to you. If it tells you that you look your fifty-seven years, then by God you do. And if there's something you want to do, somewhere you want to go, then you'd better start the doing and the going. You'd better start using the time that's left in you, because you can't stop it from running out. You can stop water from running out of a tub by putting the plug back in, but there isn't any plug that can stop time from running out of you. Oh, you can slow it down. By living right. By letting the medics give you the works in geriatrics you can baby yourself past the century mark, but brother you're still old at seventy.

In thirteen years I'd be seventy, I thought. Maybe *I'd* be old sooner than that, what with the way I'd lived most of the time, what with one foot—hell, one leg up to the knee—in the grave already.

9

It's indecent and inhuman to put full length mirrors in bathroom doors. They cause narcissism in the young and unhappiness in the old.

After I dried myself and before I put my prosthetic leg back on, I hopped up on the bathroom scale and weighed myself. A hundred and twenty-six. Not too bad, I thought; I'd gained back seven of the fourteen pounds I'd lost. If I took even reasonable care of myself I'd have the rest of it back in another few weeks and I didn't have to stay here until I had all of it back.

I looked at myself in the mirror again and this time it wasn't so bad. It still had strength in it, that body, the wiry strength that's better in the long run than heavy musculature. And now that the magnelite leg was back on it was a whole body, or looked like one.

The face above it wasn't bad either; it too had a kind of strength in it.

I dressed and went downstairs, but I didn't tell them yet. I waited until after dinner, until after Merlene went upstairs to put Easter and Bill Junior to bed. I knew there'd be an argument and I didn't want the kids in on it. Bill Senior and Merlene I could handle; I could just agree with everything they said but tell them I was leaving anyway. But what can you do with *Uncle Max, please don't go* stuff from kids.

Bill sat watching the viddy.

My kid brother, Bill. My kid brother with graying hair and a bald spot and no imagination. But a nice guy. Happily married, although he'd married late. A good steady job, good steady opinions.

But no taste whatsoever. He liked cowboy music. He was sitting listening to it now.

Out of space it came, that program. From Earth's second artificial satellite, from the telestation twenty-two thousand miles out in empty space, revolving around Earth once a day as Earth turns once a day under and with it, staying always over Kansas, always twenty-two thousand miles over the tall corn of Kansas.

In full color, that program, tri-dimensional and out of space to Earth. And it was a man in a cowboy hat strumming a guitar and singing in a Texas accent:

> Give me the lone pray-ree,
> And a stallion wild and free . . .

I'd rather have given him a gelding than a stallion, but I'd have given him anything to shut up.

Bill liked it.

I wandered over to the picture window and stood looking out into the night. A fine view of Seattle, Bill had, from this window facing it and thirty miles away, atop a hill. A fine view especially on a clear night like this one, one of those rare but wonderful warm, bright evenings that can happen in the fall of the year.

Below, the lights of Seattle; above, the lights in the sky.

Behind me, a cowboy singing. Then the song ended and Bill flicked the toggle switch on the arm of his chair that cut off sound while the commercial was on.

In the sudden and blessed silence I said, "Bill, I'm leaving."

He did what I'd hoped he wouldn't do, but had known

11

that he would. He walked over and shut off the viddy completely.

Cowboy music he was giving up. Just to argue with me, to try to talk me into staying longer.

To make it worse Merlene came back into the room just then. The kids must have gone to bed without putting up even a token battle about it. I'd counted on having Bill worn down by the time Merlene came downstairs to reinforce him. Now I had both of them at once. And Merlene had heard what I'd said.

She said "No." Firmly. She sat down on the sofa and looked at me.

I said "Yes." Mildly.

"Max Andrews, you've been here less than three weeks. You're about halfway well now. You need at least another two weeks of rest and you know it."

"Not full time rest," I said. "I'll take things easy for a while."

Bill was back in his chair. He said, "Listen, Max—" I turned toward him but he bogged down. He turned to Merlene and I turned too.

Merlene said, "You're not well enough to leave here yet and you know it."

"Then I'll no doubt fall down just outside. If I do, you can drag me back in and I'll stay. Okay?"

She glared at me. Bill cleared his throat and I looked at him. He got as far as "Listen, Max—" and bogged down again.

Merlene said, "You and those itchy feet of yours."

"Just one of them itches," I told her. "Now, children, if

this argument must continue, will you please sit together so I don't get dizzy turning around to face whichever one of you is talking. Bill, will you please sit on the sofa by your wife?"

He got up and moved over. Not gracefully; he stumbled. But grace has never been one of Bill's strong points. Opposite of Merlene; she'd been a dancer before they were married and every movement she made was graceful. She could change Easter's diapers as though it were part of a ballet—and with no conscious knowledge that she was making a dance out of it; that was what made it so wonderful to watch.

Merlene said, "Please understand this, Max. We like having you here. We like *you*. It isn't as though you are imposing on us, or anything like that. And you're paying your own way, which helps the budget a lot."

"It can't help your budget," I pointed out, "when you insist on charging me cost only and figuring it down to the penny. If you'd let me pay you a flat fifty a week, as I'd suggested—"

"Will you stay two more weeks if we let you pay it that way?"

I'd walked into that one. I said, "No, darling, I'm sorry."

I counterattacked. "Listen," I said, "you're only two to one against me, but you can increase the odds. You know I'm crazy about Easter and Billy, and they can't possibly be asleep yet. Why don't you get them here too and tell them I'm leaving so they can cry about it and soften me with their salty little tears?"

Merlene glowered at me. "You—you—"

13

I grinned at Bill. "The reason she's speechless is that she was thinking about doing just that and now she can't. She was probably wondering already what pretext she could use for bringing them back downstairs." I looked at Merlene. "But it really wouldn't be fair, honey. I don't mean to me—that doesn't matter. I mean it wouldn't be fair to them. It might disturb them emotionally, and to no purpose. Because no matter how much it disturbs either them or me I'm leaving tonight. I've got to."

Bill sighed. He sat there looking at me sadly, my kid brother with his temples turning gray. He said, "I don't suppose, then, that it'll do any good to tell you I've been working at wangling you a job with Union Transport. A good job."

"I'm a rocket mech, Bill. Union Transport doesn't use rockets."

"It would be administrative work, Max. From that point of view what's the difference between rockets and stratojets?"

"I don't like stratojets. That's the difference."

"Rockets are going out, Max. And besides—my God, you can't be just a mech all your *life*."

"Why can't I? And damn it, rockets are *not* going out. Not until we get something better."

Bill laughed. "Such as sewing machines?"

I'll never live that sewing machine episode down.

I smiled back at him, though, because by now it was funny to me too. Maybe it had been funny even then. It had cost me nearly two weeks' time and nearly a thousand

14

dollars cash but a really good joke on yourself is worth at least that.

Bill cleared his throat again, but Merlene saved me. She said, "Oh, let him alone, Bill. He's going, whatever we say, so why spoil the last evening?"

I walked across the room and patted her shoulder. "My angel," I said. "Can we have a drink to that?"

For a moment she looked doubtful. I said patiently, "It's all right, darling. I am not an alcoholic—at least not in the sense that I can't do normal social drinking or even get pixilated once in a while without it 'starting me off.' Now in celebration of my imminent departure, may I mix us a round of martinis?"

She jumped up. "I'll make them, Max." She walked out of the room and her walk was a dance. Both Bill's eyes and mine followed her.

"Good gal," I told him.

"Max, why don't you get married and settle down?"

"At my age? I'm too young to settle down."

"Seriously."

"I'm serious."

Bill shook his head slowly. Well, that's the way I felt about him and his way of life.

Merlene spared us pitying one another further by bringing in the drinks. We touched glasses.

"Luck to you, Max," Merlene said. "Decided where you're going."

"San Francisco."

"Rocket mech on Treasure Island again?"

"Probably, but not right away. I meant what I said about resting up a little first."

"But why not stay here until you're ready to go back to work?"

"Something happening there I want to look in on, maybe give a hand with. News item I heard on the viddy last night."

Bill said, "Bet I know which item. That crazy dame who's running for senator and wants to send a rocket to Jupiter. My God, *Jupiter*. What have Mars and Venus got us?"

My poor little brother, my poor brother who was rich in money and bereft of vision, my blind blind brother.

I said, "Listen, children, I'm going to catch the two A. M. jet plane. And it's only eight o'clock now, so that's six hours away. Here's a suggestion. You two haven't taken advantage of having an expert baby sitter since I've been here and this is your last chance. Why don't you rev up the hellie and run into Seattle for an evening out. Night club or something, see some live entertainment. If you get back by one-thirty or so Bill can run me to the stratoport in plenty of time to make the plane."

Merlene looked reproachful. "Your last evening here and you think we'd rather—"

"Whatever you'd rather," I told her, "*I'd* rather you did. I've got some thinking to do and some planning. And some packing. Off with you."

I talked them into it.

16

§

My suitcase by the door, ready. It wasn't heavy; I travel lightly and live lightly. Physical possessions tie you down and God knows we're tied down enough without them.

I went back upstairs to my bedroom, or to the room that had been my bedroom for the past three weeks and which was the guest room again now that all my things were out of it. This time I didn't turn on the light. I tiptoed across the room quietly—as I had packed quietly, because it was right next to the room Billy and Easter were sleeping in—opened the window and stepped through it onto the railed upper porch.

It was a beautiful night. Warm and clear. Mount Ranier in the distance, the near distance.

Overhead and in the far distance the lights in the sky that are stars. The stars they tell us we can never reach because they are too far away. They lie; we'll get there. If rockets won't take us, *something* will.

There's got to be an answer.

We got to the moon, didn't we? And Mars and Venus—

Thank God I was in on that, back in the glorious sixties when man erupted suddenly into space, the first step, the first three steps toward the stars.

I was there, I was in on it. Spaceman First Class Max Andrews.

And now? What are we doing now to reach the stars?

The stars—listen, do you know what a star is?

Our sun is a star and all the stars in the sky are suns. We know now that most of them have planets revolving about them, as Earth and Mars and Venus and the other planets of the solar system revolve around our sun.

And there are a hell of a lot of stars.

That isn't profanity; it's understatement. There are about a thousand million stars in our own galaxy. A thousand million stars, most of them with planets. If they average only one planet apiece that's a thousand million planets. If one out of a thousand of those planets happens to be Earth-type—one with a breathable atmosphere, about the same size and distance from its sun as Earth so its temperature and gravity would be similar—then there ought to be at least a million planets in our own galaxy which man can colonize and on which he can live a normal life, on which he can be fruitful and multiply.

A million worlds for us to reach and take and live on.

But that's going to be only the start, the beginning. That's only *our own galaxy,* as tiny in relation to the universe as our little solar system is to our galaxy.

There are a hell of a lot of galaxies. There are more galaxies of stars in the universe than there are stars in our own galaxy. At least a thousand million times a thousand million suns.

A million times a million planets, habitable by man. Do you know how that figures out? To twenty-five planets or so apiece for every member of the human race, every man, woman and child.

Since no one can populate a planet all by himself let's

say fifty planets per couple. Fifty planets, and if we hold the average population density down to three billion per planet, times fifty—we'll have to get there first of course, but when we do it's going to take a lot of multiplying to populate all those worlds. Well, the human race has always been good at that, hasn't it?

Or maybe we'll find some of them already populated. Well, that will be interesting too. Just *what* will they be populated with?

§

San Francisco at three-fifteen in the morning. The damn stratojet was late. They always are.

I bought a tabloid at the jetport on Angel Island and caught a helicab to Union Square, the only place right downtown where they'll let the hellies land. To try my strength I walked up Knob Hill to the Mark; it winded me a little but not too badly.

The Mark's an old hotel, run-down, and cheap—you can get a single for as little as fifteen a day. When I was a kid it was famous for its view of the harbor and the bridges; now there are mostly higher buildings around it. But if you can get a room above the seventh floor and on the California-Mason corner you can still see northeast over the low buildings of the Chinese section and you can see Treasure Island, where the rockets land. Maybe there'd be one going out or coming in tonight and even from a distance the sight of a rocket taking off or landing in the dark

19

is a beautiful thing. I hadn't seen a rocket for some months now and I was lonesome for the sight of one. I'd been away from them too long. So I asked for a high room in the right corner of the building.

The clerk told me they didn't have one there, but for ten bucks he looked again and told me someone had checked out an hour ago, in the middle of the night, and that if I wanted to take a room that hadn't been made up yet I could have it. I took it.

The room was a mess all right; the someone who'd just checked out had been a couple and obviously they'd done a lot of drinking and had had a fight in addition to using the bed and several of the towels. They'd got their money's worth even if they'd stayed only half the night.

But I didn't give a damn about that. I pulled a chair over to the window and sat there, keeping watch on the lights of Treasure and the sky over it while I read the tabloid I'd bought on Angel. Skimmed it, rather, since there wasn't anything in it on what I was interested in, the special election.

I put it down after a while and just watched for a rocket, and I thought about a lot of things. I thought about Bill's son, Billy. At six, he still had the Dream; he still wanted to be a spaceman. He wanted the stars. I wondered if I'd helped make him that way or whether it had been space opera on the viddy, and then I decided that it didn't matter. As long as he had the Dream, and if he kept it. One more starduster he'd be. One more crackpot. And every one of us counts. When there are enough of us—

Fog began to drift over the harbor as the sky grayed

with dawn and I knew I wouldn't be able to see a rocket any more if one took off or landed, so I went to sleep. There in the chair, not wanting to lie in or even on that rumpled messy bed. But I slept soundly.

§

The maid woke me, trying the door.

There was bright sunshine out the window and my wrist watch told me it was eleven o'clock and that I must have slept about seven hours. I was stiff when I got up out of the chair.

But I went to the door before she got away and told her I was going out for a short while and would appreciate it if she cleaned the room. Stiff, dirty and unshaven, I went downstairs for breakfast. Cleaning up and shaving could wait till the bathroom was cleaned up and had fresh towels. I wondered if the maid would think I messed up the room like that and then I decided it didn't matter what she thought.

When I came back the room was clean and orderly and I took a shower and shaved. The stiffness was gone and I decided I felt pretty good.

I phoned Treasure Island and asked for the head mech, Rory Bursteder. His voice came on and I said, "This is Max, Rory. How's everything?"

He said, "Max who?"

"Max No Difference," I told him.

Rory roared, "Max Andrews! You son of a bitch you, where you been the last year?"

"Here and there. Mostly New Orleans."

"Where you calling from?"

I told him.

"Get the hell over here fast. Start you right in."

I said, "I don't want to start work for about a week yet, Rory. Something I want to look into here, first."

"Oh. The election, maybe?"

"Yeah. I just heard about it yesterday, up in Seattle. What's the score?"

"Come on over and I'll tell you. Or—wait a minute, got any plans for this evening?"

"Nope."

"Then eat with me and the old lady. We're still in Berkeley so this is halfway there for you. I'm off at six; meet me at the gate then and we'll go the rest of the way together."

"Swell," I said. "But listen, what take-offs or landings are there this afternoon?"

"Only one. Paris rocket takes off at five-fifteen. Okay, I'll leave word at the gate to get you in at five."

§

Rory's wife Bess is a wonderful cook. Not that I hadn't enjoyed the meals at Bill's, but Merlene is a little on the fancy side as a cook, worries as much about how a dish looks as how it tastes. Bess Bursteder's cooking is old-

22

fashioned and German, but she makes dumplings so light they need the thick rich gravy to keep them from rising off the plate and floating away, and the meat was so tender that it must have come from Circassian virgins, young ones.

We washed it down with ale and then sat back and relaxed. I couldn't have got up if I'd wanted to.

I said, "Now tell me about the election deal, Rory."

"Well—it looks like a fair chance."

"That's not what I meant, although I want to hear that too. Listen, all I heard was a few sentences of a newscast yesterday. All I know is some dame named Gallagher is running for senator from California and if she gets in she plans to introduce and back a bill making an appropriation to cover an expedition to go around Jupiter."

"That's right."

"But damn it, that's *all* I know. What are the details? First, how come a special election? I thought the governor of a state could appoint someone to finish the unexpired term of a senator who dies while in office."

"You're ten years out of date. Revised Statutes of nineteen eighty-seven—if a senatorship is vacated by death with more than half of the unexpired term remaining a special election must be held at a date to be set before the next session of Congress."

"Oh. Well, that answers that. Now, who the hell is this Gallagher woman?"

"Ellen Gallagher, forty-five, widow of Ralph Gallagher who died while he was mayor of Los Angeles six or seven years ago. She struck out on her own in politics after that

—she'd been active in them before, but only to work in her husband's interests. Two terms in the California assembly since then, now running for senator. Next question."

"What makes her tick? Is she a starduster?"

"No. But she's a friend of Bradly of Caltech. Know of him?"

"I've read some of his stuff. A little stodgy, but good."

"One of us, within limitations. He still kowtows to the relativists, thinks we'll never exceed the speed of light. But anyway he sold the Gallagher dame on the Jupiter run—only hell, why didn't she keep her hatch shut about it until after she got in? California's pretty conservationist and jetting off may cost her the election."

"We'll have to see it doesn't. Who's bucking her?"

"Guy named Layton, Dwight Layton, of Sacramento. Ex-mayor there and has a machine. Crooked as they come. Conservationist."

I shuddered. "Is that all?"

"He's buying a lot of viddy time and he's a smooth talker. He says mankind is wasting his most valuable resource, uranium, spending it in prodigious quantities to maintain valueless minor colonies on a dead moon and dead Mars. Earth is impoverishing itself in the futile effort to make a long-since-proved-impractical dream come true. Over a hundred billion dollars spent on Mars alone, and what is there of value to us on Mars? Sand and lichens, not enough air to support human life, bitter cold. Yet we spend more millions every year to supply a few dozen people who are mad enough to try—"

"Shut up," I said. "That's enough."

Bess said, "Scram, you boys. I want to clear the table."

We helped her. Afterward, over some ale in the living room, I said to Rory, "All right, I've got the picture now. What can I do about it?"

He sighed. "Well—to start with, you can vote. Got here just in time to register; tomorrow's the last day. You'll have to come over to Berkeley again to do it because you'll have to claim a year's residence to vote, see, and you can give this address; we'll say you've been rooming with us that long."

"Good," I said.

Bess said, "Except that it's silly for you to go back across the bay tonight and then come back here just to register. Stay with us tonight and register in the morning before you go back."

"Swell; thanks, Bess."

Rory said, "Should have thought of that myself. Well, to get back to what you can do about the election; you've got plenty of friends in San Francisco so you can register in a few precincts over there. You can probably be set to cast three or four votes next Tuesday."

"Can do. Five or six maybe."

"And make sure your friends have registered. We don't have to worry which way they'd vote, or they wouldn't be friends of yours. And every vote will help, Max."

"Sure, every vote will help. But even if I can swing a couple of dozen votes that's peanuts. Damn it, isn't there anything more than that?"

"Damn if I know what, Max. You're no speaker. If you get yourself a soap box or even buy viddy time, you'll get

25

het up and sound like a fanatic—which you are—and probably alienate more people than you'll convince."

I sighed. "'Fraid you're right on that. Still, maybe there's *something*. I can look up the Gallagher and ask her—like to meet her anyway."

"Don't think she's in town. But you could look up her campaign manager. Richard Shearer. Got a suite at the St. Francis for campaign quarters. I talked to him on the phone yesterday."

"What about?"

"Heard he was going to send a speaker over to Treasure to talk to the boys during lunch hour. Told him not to waste the speaker; he had the Treasure Island vote solid anyway and might as well send the guy where it could help him."

"Right," I said. "I'll see him first thing Thursday; I'll spend tomorrow getting registered myself and making sure my friends are."

§

I set my alarm for half past three on Thursday. Not to see Richard Shearer that early, but because the Moscow rocket was due to land at three-forty, the first rocket to land or take off at night since I'd been there. Night rocket flights are relatively infrequent; why risk night landings when a few hours will take you as far as a terrestrial rocket need go in one flight, halfway around the earth? But night landings are beautiful to watch.

26

From the window, standing there in my room in the dark, I watched it. You've seen a rocket sit down on its fiery tail; I don't have to describe it for you. It's the most wonderful fireworks that ever were, the fireworks that gave us the moon and Mars and Venus and that can and will take us to other and farther planets.

Rockets are going out, Bill had said.

They *are* going out, but not far enough. We took the first steps and then we lost our guts. Temporarily—it *must* be temporarily—we've lost our drive, or most of us have.

Not all of us, thank God, not all. Millions of us, millions besides me, want the stars. But right now there are more millions who don't—or who mildly do but think it's impossible anyway in our lifetimes, and that it's not worth the money it would cost to try.

Worst of all there are the reactionaries, the conservationists, the shortsighted tightwads with no vision at all, who think everything we have done is wasted time and effort just because it hasn't yet yielded any financial return.

Of course they haven't, but they're only steps, the first steps, and even when we took them we knew from our astronomers what to expect to find there. But Jesus, when you're climbing a staircase to a room—an infinite room—filled with all the treasures of the universe, should you stop climbing just because you don't find a handful of treasure on the first two or three steps?

Conservationists, millions of them, calling us crackpots, stardusters. Taxes they worry about, money they worry about. We've gone into debt enough, they say, and why go any farther? The planets are worthless and the stars—why, if we can reach them at all, it might take us thousands of years.

I'll buy part of that. It *may* take us thousands of years, and it damn well will unless we keep trying with everything we've got. But if we do keep trying it can happen suddenly too. It can come as unexpectedly as our reaching Mars came in 1965, four years ahead of our schedule for reaching the moon. Suddenly we'd found the A-drive and the chemicals fuels we'd been working with and figuring on were obsolete. We were in the situation of a man trying to cross the ocean in a rowboat, when only a few miles out from shore he is suddenly given a supersonic-speed airplane to use instead of his rowboat.

Maybe it'll be the same way when we try for the stars, for let's face it that even an A-drive rocket is a rowboat when it comes to interstellar distances. We may find something new that will make the stars as relatively easy as the A-drive made the planets, but damn it, we'll find it only when we're *trying*, all out, to get there with what we've got. Like we were *trying* for the moon, all out, with chemical rockets when we found the A-drive.

§

At nine o'clock I walked into Suite 1315 of the St. Francis. *Gallagher for Senator Headquarters*, the sign on the door read. A blonde receptionist was spreading papers around on her desk. She looked up when I came in and

28

liked what she saw or she'd been told to smile at everybody; anyway, she smiled.

I thought I'd first check Rory's information that the candidate herself wasn't in town. "Is Ellen Gallagher in?"

"Mrs. Gallagher won't be in. She's on a speaking tour in the northern part of the state. I'm sorry."

"Why should you be sorry? Richard Shearer in?"

"He'll be in any moment. Would you care to sit down and—Oh, here he is. This gentleman wants to see you, Mr. Shearer."

The man who'd just come in was a big redhead with a moon face. I introduced myself and he shook hands. "What can I do for you, Mr. Andrews?" His voice was deep and slow, almost a drawl.

"Tell me how I can help Ellen Gallagher get elected."

"Come in my office." He led the way to an inner room, showed me a chair and sat at a desk, one of the old-type all-plastic automatics.

"You're a friend of Mrs. Gallagher's, Mr. Andrews?"

"Sure," I said. "I've never met her, but if she's going to back an appropriation for a rocket to Jupiter I'm a friend of hers."

"Oh, a starduster." He grinned. "Well, we can use starduster support; in fact, we'll certainly need it now that our candidate has stuck her neck out about that rocket."

"Which you don't approve of?"

"I approve of the rocket. I think it's about time we tried another step out. But I'm afraid her statement to the press about it, just before the election, was a political mistake that will cost her more votes than it will win her."

"Enough to lose her the election?"

"I don't know, Mr. Andrews. But we'll certainly need the solid starduster vote, now that we're committed."

I said, "Don't worry about the starduster vote. You'll get it—several times over in at least some cases."

He smiled faintly. "I'm afraid to ask you just what you mean by that, so let's forget it, or still better let's say I didn't hear you."

"All right, I didn't say it. But you just said you didn't *know* whether she'd win. What do you *think?*"

He was silent so long that I decided to say it for him. "So she's going to lose, as things stand."

"I'm afraid it does look that way. Unless something unexpected happens—"

"Such as a sudden and unexpected accident to this Dwight Layton?"

He'd been slouching forward on his desk. Now he sat up straight as suddenly as though someone had just pushed a ramrod up him.

He said, "You're not suggesting—" He stared at me. "By Christ I believe you are and I believe you'd try to *arrange* one."

"Consider it a hypothetical question but answer it. Would it help Gallagher's chances?"

He got up and started pacing the length of the office slowly, thinking. Five times, and then he stopped and faced me. "No, it would be the worst thing that could happen for her—even if Layton had a *genuine* accident."

"Why?"

"Because Dwight Layton is a damned crook, although

30

nobody can prove it. But plenty of people, even in his own party, suspect it, and it's going to cost him some votes. Not as many, I'm afraid, as Ellen's unfortunate statement is going to cost her, but it'll help. With any other candidate bucking her—even someone run in at the last minute whom the public had never heard of, she'd have even less chance. Besides, if Layton had an accident of such a nature that there could be even a remote suspicion that it had been arranged by a fanatical starduster—my God, man, don't you see the damage that would do to *your* cause, all over the country, besides what it would do to Ellen?"

"You're right," I said. "Forget it. In what way is Layton a crook? What's he done?"

"As mayor of Sacramento, he got rich awfully suddenly. The rumor is that it was kickbacks on public construction contracts. But it's covered up damned well. The income tax boys investigated him last year on the strength of the rumors and had to give him a clean bill of health."

"Must have a good accountant."

"He *is* a good accountant. Was near the top in that field before he got into politics. He's clever, and there isn't a thing against him. If we even intimate there is, he can sue the bejesus out of us."

"What if *I* intimate it? Hire viddy time with my own money, having no connection with the Gallagher campaign? What if I accuse him openly and don't mind being sued?"

He shook his head slowly. "It would still react against Ellen. You can't attack one candidate in an election without automatically associating yourself with the other one.

31

No, I'm afraid there's not a thing you can do, Mr. Andrews, that won't do us more harm than good. Nothing on a large scale, that is. Of course we'll appreciate your vote and whatever votes you can swing among your friends."

And he held out his hand to me, showing the interview was over.

§

I wandered around a while, thinking. I wanted to do some thinking, plenty of it, before I settled for anything as weak as voting a few times myself and helping swing a few or even a few dozen other votes. Even a few hundred votes wouldn't help much, the way her campaign manager had talked when he'd finally leveled with me.

I found myself passing Union Square. There was a platform in the middle and a guy on it talking; his voice was amplified and you could hear it all over the square.

"*Jupiter*," he said, as though it was a swear word. "This woman proposes to spend our money—and it would take at least a billion dollars of it—to send a rocket around Jupiter. A billion dollars that we'll have to pay, money out of our pockets, bread out of our mouths!

"A billion dollars, and what are we buying for it? Another worthless planet? Not even that. Just a closer *look* at another worthless planet. The rocket wouldn't even land. It couldn't land."

There was a small crowd around the platform, but people all over the square, passing on every side of it, were listening, hearing, even though they walked on about their business.

I thought of going up to the platform, climbing up on it and slapping him silly. My hands itched to do it. But it wouldn't help and it would only land me in jail so I couldn't even vote myself.

So I didn't. For once I was sensible.

"The planet *Jupiter*. Four hundred million miles away, more than *eight times* as far as Mars, a planet on which man can never land. It has a poisonous atmosphere of methane and ammonia, so thick that at the bottom it is liquid under pressures so great that the strongest rocket would be crushed like an eggshell, an atmosphere thousands of miles deep and in constant turbulence. Below that atmosphere? A layer thousands of miles thick, under terrific pressure. Our telescopes tell us these things about Jupiter, tell us that it is not fit for man. We already know that this giant planet has so strong a gravitational pull that a spaceship cannot even approach it closely without crashing—or should I say splashing?—into it. We already know that its moons are more barren, colder, more inhospitable than our own. And yet Mrs. Gallagher wants to waste a billion dollars of our money to . . ."

Hands balled in my pockets, I made myself stand there quietly and listen, just so I'd get mad enough to try to do what I'd decided would give Ellen Gallagher her only chance to win the election.

§

It was noon when I got to Sacramento. The jetport was jammed—I think it was because of a convention of some kind—and I had a lot of trouble getting a helicab into town. But by half past one I was in front of the building on K Street in which Dwight Layton had his office suite.

A minute later I was in the outer office of the suite.

The receptionist was tough, but not too tough; I fast-talked my way past her on the story that my business was highly personal and that it concerned the campaign and seriously affected Mr. Layton's chances. And no, it wasn't anything I could take up with his campaign manager or his secretary or anybody but Mr. Layton himself.

He was busy just then and I had to wait twenty-seven minutes, but I got in.

I gave him a phony name and started an excited crack-pot spiel about unfair tactics that the God damned star-dusters were using against him in the campaign. Still talking excitedly, I let him ease me out within a minute.

I could have held out longer, but a minute had been long enough for me to get a look at the layout of his office, the kinds of locks on the inner and outer doors, and the make and size of his safe. It was a big but old-fashioned job that any good mech could open in ten minutes with the right tools.

I bought all the things I'd need and a brief case to carry them in. I killed time until nine o'clock and then burgled Layton's office.

No burglar alarm; that's the one chance I'd taken.

I didn't even have to open the safe. I tried the desk first.

34

It had one locked drawer and in the drawer, the only thing in it, was a red ledger. The entries in it were in Layton's handwriting—I compared it with the writing on other papers in the desk to make sure. Names, dates and amounts, even notations of what sales to the city of Sacramento they represented percentages of. Enough evidence to send him to jail half a dozen times over.

Strange and systematic is the mind of an accountant.

There might have been money in the safe and it wouldn't have hurt my conscience to take it, but I didn't want to risk tarrying. I had what I'd come for and it was more important than money. I didn't want to crowd my luck.

I mailed it in a plain wrapper to Richard Shearer at the St. Francis.

I went back to San Francisco and to bed.

§

Just before noon I phoned Shearer.

"Did you get a package?" I asked him.

"God yes. Who is this?"

"The man who sent it. Leave us name no names, particularly over the telephone. Have you done anything with it yet?"

"I'm still deciding the best way to use it. I'm sweating."

"Quit sweating," I said. "Turn it over to the state police, that's all. But in front of an office full of reporters, to whom

35

you furnish photographic copies of a few of the juiciest pages."

"But where do I say I got it?"

"Where *did* you get it? It was mailed to you in a plain wrapper from Sacramento. You can turn the wrapper over to the cops too. It hasn't any fingerprints on it and the address is in block lettering. Your hunch is that somebody in Layton's organization hates his guts. And that's what Layton himself will probably figure, if that matters. He won't find any evidence of a burglary and he probably hasn't even missed it yet."

"Listen, what do you want out of this? What can we do for you?"

"You can do two things for me. The first is to buy me a drink and over that I'll tell you the second. I'll be in the Big Dipper Bar in fifteen minutes. I'll know you if you don't know me."

"I think I'll know you. Didn't you imply in my office yesterday that you were going to vote several times?"

"Quiet," I said. "Don't you know that voting more than once is against the law?"

I'd picked the Big Dipper for its name; I'd been past it but had never gone in. It turned out to be a nice quiet spot, though. I took a booth and a few minutes later Shearer came in.

He looked both excited and worried. He said, "I guess your suggestion about the state police, with reporters watching, is the best bet. I'd thought of it too. But I'll wait until tomorrow, Saturday, late in the day; that'll break it in the Saturday evening newscasts and the Sunday papers, and give it the best coverage. It'll be a shoo-in, a boat race."

"How will you account for the delay? The postmark shows you got it today."

"Easy. I still don't know whether it's the McCoy or not. How do I know if that's really Layton's handwriting or if someone is trying to hoax me out on a limb?"

I frowned. "You don't really think there's a possibility I'm pulling something like that on you, do you?"

"Hell, no. But if it had really come to me cold, as I'm going to have to tell it, I'd have been plenty suspicious. Anyway it's going to take me until tomorrow afternoon to make sure and some photographs will be taken in the process; that's how come I'll have them on hand for the reporters. Okay, what's the one thing you want besides this drink?"

"It can wait till after the election. Ellen Gallagher will be busy until then. But I want you to tell her who really got you that ledger and fix an appointment with her for me. Think she'll talk to me?"

"Talk to you? Man, she ought to sleep with you. Okay, what else?"

"Nothing you can promise me. I'll have a favor to ask the Gallagher. That's why I want her to know I've got one coming."

He sipped his drink and looked at me. "You can't ride that rocket, you know, even if Ellen would want you to. Top age for pilots—"

I held up a hand to stop him. "Do you think I'm crazy? I know better than you do what the top age for spacemen

37

is. Thirty, and I'm fifty-seven. No, I can't ride it. But I can help push it and that's all I want."

He nodded. "I know Ellen well enough to say she'll get you the best job on the project you're qualified for. If it goes through, of course; I wouldn't give it over one chance out of ten myself."

"What chance would you have given Ellen Gallagher to be elected, up to the time you got that ledger?"

"About the same. But getting a bill through Congress is something else again. You can't burgle the office of every congressman who's going to vote against it."

I grinned at him. I said, "I can try."

§

The election was a shoo-in, a boat race. The story had broken at just the right time and both viddy and the papers had made the most of it. Layton's party had made a desperate last-minute effort; Layton himself had appeared on the viddy claiming innocence but announcing his withdrawal from the race until he could clear himself of the charges against him, in favor of someone else whose name nobody bothered to listen to. The last-minute substitute carried six precincts in Sacramento and Ellen Gallagher carried everything else.

At eight o'clock that evening Bess, Rory and I watched the opposition concede defeat. We left the viddy on, turned low, because we all wanted to see Ellen Gallagher and hear what she had to say. It had been announced that she was leaving Los Angeles to fly to San Francisco by stratojet and would be interviewed on its landing at Angel Island at eight thirty-seven.

Bess got the bottle of champagne from the refrigerator; we'd held off opening it until the election had been formally conceded.

We poured drinks around and toasted victory.

We drank and talked. At thirty-five minutes after eight I saw the viddy screen switch to an interviewer at the jetport so I went over and turned up the sound.

". . . very thick fog," he was saying. "Visibility is just about zero out there on the field so we'll wait until Senator Gallagher is inside here to interview her. You wouldn't be able to see the jet land anyway; it will have to come in on instruments. But it's coming down now, exactly on time. I can hear it."

I said, "My God, Rory, those jets are lousy on instrument landings. What if—"

And we heard the crash.

I started to rush out to go there but Rory pulled me back. He said, "We'll get the news here quicker."

It came in gradually, a piece at a time. The plane had cracked up badly, many of the passengers had been killed outright and none of them had escaped injury. The co-pilot had survived and was conscious when they pulled him out. He said that both the radar and the radio had gone out simultaneously when they were only yards off the ground, too late to pull up again.

One at a time they got the others out. Richard Shearer,

39

Mrs. Gallagher's campaign manager, dead. Dr. Emmett Bradly of Caltech, dead.

"God damned stratojet," Rory said.

The Gallagher was alive. Unconscious and badly injured, but alive. She was being rushed to the Angel Island emergency hospital and further reports on her condition would be given as soon as possible.

Wailing of ambulance sirens in the fog. Damn San Francisco, damn fogs, damn stratojets, damn everything.

We sat and waited. The champagne was warm and flat. Rory poured it out in the sink and got us cold beer instead. I didn't touch mine.

It was after eleven before there was further word on Senator Gallagher. She was alive and expected to live, but very seriously injured. Two operations had been performed. She would be hospitalized for months. But eventual recovery was reasonably certain.

I wondered if Richard Shearer had told her yet the real story of how he'd got the ledger. He *must* have. She'd certainly have asked him about it and he'd have had no reason to stall on telling her—except that he might not have been alone with her and he couldn't have told her in front of others.

Yes, it could all too easily have happened. She'd had a party of seven with her, five others besides Shearer, who had flown down to join her only that afternoon in Los Angeles, and Bradly. It was all too possible she hadn't been alone with Shearer.

Finally I drank the glass of beer Rory had poured for

me. It was as warm by then as the champagne had been, and flatter.

The next morning I started working at Treasure Island under Rory.

1998

1998

WORKING on rockets. Working on rockets that were going out, but not far enough out. Only a few hundred miles out, these rockets, and then back to Earth again. The rockets for New York and Paris and Moscow and Tokyo and Brisbane and Johannesburg and Janeiro. Not even for the moon or Mars, these rockets out of San Francisco. Those rockets, the *real* rockets, take off from bases in New Mexico and Arizona. The government runs them, and the government has silly ideas about rocket mechs. The government thinks rocket mechs should not be over fifty. The govern-

§

ment thinks rocket mechs should have both legs made of flesh and bone. Oh, I've worked on the interplanetaries despite that latter ruling, times when friends of mine have been in position to get me special dispensation on the leg. But not since I'd passed the fifty mark seven years ago; that's one rule that's really enforced at the government bases. A few times since I passed fifty I've worked short periods at the interplanetary bases, but not as a rocket mech, not working on the rockets but just to be near them, to see them, to touch one occasionally and to watch take-offs and landings. But never for long periods; there's no future, no pathway to the stars, in working in a commissary or being a feather merchant. It's better actually to work on rockets, even if they're only the terrestrial ones that take off from Earth to come down again.

So, San Francisco—and besides, Senator Gallagher was there. Still in the hospital, but now recovering. She'd live all right, my gal whom I'd never met. She'd live and be completely well in a few months, just a matter of time. Just a matter of time to Jupiter, the next outward step. Just a matter of time, and time running out.

Oh, I accomplished something that January. I got an idea that slightly cut down the weight of a gyro-stabilizer. I got a thousand-dollar bonus for it and it would save the terrestrial rocket lines quite a few thousand a year. That wasn't important, though; the important thing was that the improvement could be and would be used on the interplanetaries too. A tiny saving in mass-ratio, an inch closer to the stars. That's what mattered. Rory and Bess and I spent a hundred of my thousand bonus on a spree.

§

The good news, the big news, came a few weeks later, in February. A letter from Senator Gallagher, at last. I was moving around a bit, hadn't yet found quarters I really liked, so I was getting my mail at the Bursteders', and Bess called me at work one day to tell me the letter had come. Of course I told her to tear it open and read it quick. Pause for tearing envelope, unfolding letter.

"*Dear Mr. Andrews,*" Bess read: "*At long last I am allowed to dictate answers to some of the letters I have received, and yours is of course among the first.*

"*Yes Ricky Shearer told me it was you who supplied the bombshell that won me the election and I am deeply aware of my indebtedness to you. His telling me was, as it happened, one of the last acts of his life; we were sitting together in the stratojet and he told me just as we were coming in for the landing at Angel.*

"*It is not yet certain, although the doctors are hopeful, whether or not I shall take my place in the current session of Congress, which will probably adjourn in May this year, but I shall certainly be completely recovered by midsummer and more than ready for the nineteen ninety-nine session starting next January.*

"*Meanwhile, and long before then, I hope to meet you and to be able to discuss the Jupiter project with you. Yes, I know your interest is in the project and not in me personally, and I shall do my best to push that project and, if at all possible, to give you an active part in it if the appropriation is approved. I know that is what you want and I know that it is the only adequate way I can thank you for what you did for me in the election campaign.*

"*I shall write you again, probably in about a month. By that time I shall be able to have visitors and hope you will be able to call on me.*"

"Wonderful," I told Bess.

And wonderful I meant. I was still in. Dear Richard Shearer, Ricky, had come through. He'd lived long enough to tell the Gallagher the truth about that ledger. Dear Ricky, I loved him. I loved everybody. I was still in.

§

And the rockets still went out and I worked on them. Up they went, even though down they came, down to other cities two thousand miles or more away. That's the minimum distance it's worth while sending a local rocket. You can't take off and land one in much less than that. And if you could the time saving over a stratojet plane wouldn't be great enough to matter much.

Even on short hauls like New York and Mexico City the saving in time is only a few hours. Let's face it that there's no *great* saving in time on runs shorter than, say, the Paris run. That takes eighteen hours by stratojet, with the two refueling stops it has to make, and less than four hours by rocket. Fourteen hours is worth saving, but even so only the rich can afford to save it because the rocket fare is more than ten times as much. Thank God for the rich. Thank God for the rich because they keep the local rockets going. And it's important that they be kept going because the interplanetaries, the ones that really matter, benefit by every small technical improvement that the operators of the locals make, and there have been thousands of such improvements. Not big ones, mostly, but each one of them counts because it will add however slightly to the pay load an interplanetary job can carry. Or cut the time of its journey by a few minutes or increase its safety factor by a fraction of a percent. Not to mention that the locals give jobs to rocket mechs who because of age or some other silly technicality can't work on the government jobs. All the puddle-jumper operators care about is whether you're technically qualified and physically able to do the work.

Yes, thank God for the rich.

§

Senator Gallagher didn't write a second time. She phoned instead, one evening in late March. She still had Rory's address for me and called there; luckily I was spending the evening with them so the call didn't have to be relayed.

Bess answered the phone. "For you, Max," she told me. "A strange woman. Maybe it's—"

And it was.

"Mr. Andrews? This is Ellen Gallagher. I'm home now and feeling much better. I'm allowed visitors, with half an hour time limit. Would it be convenient for you to call soon?"

"Any time," I told her. "Right now, for that matter—or wait, you say you're home again. Does that mean you're calling from Los Angeles?"

"No, I'm still in San Francisco. By 'home' I mean an apartment I've taken here for a month or two so I can stay in close touch with the doctor who's been treating me. It's on Telegraph Hill."

"If tonight's okay, I can be there in half an hour."

She laughed. It was a nice laugh; I was going to like her. Like her? Hell, I loved her already. She said, "You really are in a hurry, Mr. Andrews. And you sound and talk just as Ricky described you. But I really shouldn't have company tonight. Are you free tomorrow? Could you come at about two in the afternoon?"

I told her I was free and would see her then—and of course I was free as soon as I explained to Rory and arranged with him to knock off work at noon. That would give me plenty of time after lunch to clean up, dress up and get there.

§

A private nurse let me into the apartment and took me to the room where Ellen Gallagher was sitting up in bed, waiting for me.

She looked pale but prettier than the pictures of her I'd seen; maybe that was because the only pictures I'd run across were black-and-whites and her chestnut hair, almost red, was much more striking than it had photographed. She didn't look forty-five, either; she could have passed for anywhere in the thirties. Her eyes were dark, wide apart. Her mouth, too, was wide and generous. On second thought, second look, she wasn't pretty; I'd used the wrong word there. But she was attractive, and she was all woman.

"Not bad," I said.

She laughed. "Thank you, Mr. Andrews."

"Max to you, Ellen," I said.

"All right, Max. Sit down and quit pacing like that. The rocket isn't ready to take off yet."

I hadn't known I'd been pacing. I sat down. "When?" I asked.

"You know how long a government project takes."

Yes, I knew that. I knew it would take at least a year to get started after the appropriation went through. Longer than that unless somebody behind it pushed and kept pushing. And, as a government job, at least two years to build a new type rocket. Private industry could do it in about half the time.

I asked, "What, honestly, do you think your chances are of getting it through Congress?"

"Pretty good, Max. I can make it look good, get it good publicity, get statements from all the top scientists about the value to science of a close examination of Jupiter. Of course that's window dressing. Actually, since it's a comparatively small appropriation, I'll put it through by horse trading."

"Horse trading? How do you mean?"

She looked at me and shook her head wonderingly. "You really don't know how Congress operates?"

"No. Tell me."

"It's like this, Max. Every congressman has some bill he personally wants to put through, usually something he wants to get for his home state, for his constituents, so they'll vote him back into office. Senator Cornhusker, let's say, from Iowa wants a new and higher parity price on corn. We horse trade. I vote for his bill and he votes for mine."

"Good God," I said. "There are a hundred and two senators. You mean you'll have to make a hundred and one—"

"Max, you're not thinking straight. Fifty-two votes is a majority. I can count on at least thirty-five—there are that many who'll vote for it in any case. That leaves only seventeen—or twenty to play safe—votes I'll have to trade for."

"But the House of Representatives—"

"Will be tougher. But the starduster lobby will help. They'll know exactly which votes can be counted on anyway and how to swing enough others. They'll handle the liaison work, fix it so I can trade for blocks of votes there—one vote in the senate is worth eight house votes since the last reapportionment. And I won't have to do all the trading myself, either; the lobby can line up at least a few representatives who'll want that bill through badly enough to do some trading themselves."

"That sounds like it will take time. Is there any chance of getting it through this coming session? I mean, if you get well fast enough to get there say a month before adjournment?"

She shook her head definitely. "Max, even if I hadn't been injured, even if I was there now, I wouldn't try pushing it through this session. This is ninety-eight, a presidential election year. President Jansen will run for re-election—and probably win. He's mildly on our side; he'll not veto the bill if it comes to him after re-election. But just *before* election he'd almost have to."

"What if he's not re-elected?"

"I think he will be, but it shouldn't matter too much to us if he isn't. Whoever'd beat him would be almost certain to be a middle-of-the-roader who'll approve a small expansionist bill like ours even though he'd veto, as Jansen would, any really big new move—like trying to colonize another planet or trying to build a star-ship."

"How can you be sure? Sure, I mean, that he'd be a middle-of-the-roader?"

"Because neither party would dare run a deep-dyed conservationist any more than they'd dare run a rabid starduster. Luckily the split there isn't on party lines—and the starduster vote is big enough that neither party would dare have it solidly in opposition. And be glad it's that way, Max, for right now. If party lines were drawn that way, we'd be in the minority."

"I can see that. But one thing I can't see. Woman, since you're smart enough to figure politics like that, how come you were dopey enough to let Jupiter become an issue in that special election? Telling those reporters you were going to back a new rocket damn near lost you the job."

"I know. I would have lost it except for what you did. But it wasn't really my mistake, Max. Brad—Dr. Bradly of Caltech—made it. He let it slip that he'd worked out details of the project and that I was going to back it in Congress if I got in. The reporters came to me for confirmation—and I couldn't let Brad down, could I? I couldn't call him a liar."

"No, you couldn't," I said. "But why did *he* do such a damn fool—"

"Max!" Her voice was a little sharp. "Brad's dead, remember. And anyway it was he who sold me on the project. It was his idea."

"I'm sorry," I said.

She smiled again. "All right, let's forget it. Tell me—"

She looked toward the doorway as we heard footsteps coming toward it. The nurse appeared there. "It's been half an hour, Mrs. Gallagher. You told me to remind you."

"Thanks, Dorothy." She looked back at me. "Max, what I was just going to ask you will take quite a bit of time for you to answer. So for now let's just arrange a time for you to come back."

We set it for Friday evening at seven.

§

I bought a pair of six-inch optical glass blanks to grind myself a lens for a reflecting telescope. I wanted to be able to do a lot of looking, without having to go to an observatory to do it, at Big Jupe and his moons.

I'd have lots of time to look if there wasn't a chance of the project getting started for at least another year.

I started grinding. It's a long, tedious job, but it would help pass the time for me.

§

Friday evening Ellen Gallagher was sitting up in a chair, wearing a housecoat. She looked better, less pale.

She said, "Sit down, Max. All right, we'll start where we

54

left off. I was going to bring the conversation around to you. What do you want?"

"You know damn well what I want. I want to ride that rocket. But we both know damned well that I can't, so that's that. Next to riding it, I want to help you get it through Congress, help build it, watch it take off, and then live long enough to watch it land again. I want to know that we've taken one more step out toward where we're going."

"That's what I thought. Yes, I can fix it for you to work on the rocket. But as for your helping get it through Congress—no, definitely not. That's not your department. It's my job and I can do it."

"I don't seem to recall having done too badly—"

"Max, that was different. You didn't get me elected, you know. You got my opponent defeated. Sure, the result was the same. But something like that wouldn't help a bill through Congress. What would you do? Burglarize congressmen's offices to get something to blackmail them with?"

"I could argue with people."

"Max, you'd do more harm than good in Washington. Stay away from the place. Promise me you will?"

"All right. I guess you're right."

"Good. Now about what kind of a job we can get you on the project, once it's started—well, Ricky Shearer told me you were a rocket mech and that he thought but wasn't sure that you were an ex-spaceman. Are you?"

I nodded.

"Honorable discharge? Where's your discharge button?"

"In a drawer someplace. I don't wear it. Don't feel I should wear it for something I did so many years ago."

"Start wearing it. Your having been a spaceman will help. Now start from scratch and tell me your background and your qualifications."

"All right," I said. I sighed. "Scratch was in the year nineteen hundred and forty, in Chicago, Illinois. I was the son of poor but honest parents."

"No corn, Max. Tell this straight. It may be important."

"Okay, sorry. Well, I was seventeen in fifty-seven when work was started on the space station project, the space station that was to be our first step toward the moon and then the planets.

"I was space-nutty, of course, like a few million other kids. Hell, in those days all kids were space-nutty. Of course I wanted to be a spaceman. Every seventeen-year-old in his right mind wanted to be a spaceman.

"But I was smarter than most of them because I figured out—or guessed—the right way to get in, ahead of the rush. I enlisted in the air corps, for pilot training, just before the rush started. Only a month later the word got around that when a space corps was formed, spacemen would be drawn from the air force, the pick of the best pilots would be the first chosen. And suddenly over a million kids tried to enlist in the air force all at once."

I grinned. "And of course the air force could take only a few of them and it got to be harder to get into the air force than—than to get elected to Congress. They were able to take just about one out of every thousand applicants.

"But there was I with my little piccolo, already in pilot training. And I made the grade. Got to be a hot ship pilot, a jet pilot—and knew I'd get into the space corps eventually. But not in the first class, because there were several hundred pilots ahead of me, ones who had priority over me because they'd been in the air force longer. There were three hundred in the first class at space school, the class that started in fifty-eight, while the rockets they'd be flying were still on the drafting board. Those big three-step deals, tall as a ten story building and able to lift only a few hundred pounds of pay load up to the orbit they were going to put the space station in.

"That first class, or the half of it that didn't get washed out, graduated in sixty-two. Ready, just in time, for the rockets that were ready to start putting the space station up there in the sky. But there were still more spacemen than rockets and it looked bad when I graduated in the second class in sixty-three."

I laughed. "Only the top dozen of the *first* class had ever actually got off Earth. I was near the top of my class but there were still over a hundred ahead of me. And I was getting old—I was twenty-three! In those chemical rocket days rocketing was so rough that twenty-seven was the top age for active duty and it looked like those other four years might go by before I'd get up there, even on a ferry trip to the space station! Woman, I nearly went nuts worrying."

"I'll bet you did. It could have happened."

I said, "Sure, it could have happened. But something else happened first, thank God. Nineteen sixty-four happened—and the lid blew off. So suddenly that it seemed overnight, although they'd been working on it for years, the Los Alamos boys came up with the micropile and we had atomic energy for rockets.

"Those old chemical fuel rockets were all of a sudden as obsolete as ox carts. Sure, we still needed fuel tanks but because of the high exhaust velocities atomic energy gave us, relatively small ones. And just to carry any inexpensive liquid, even water, for the micropile to turn into exhaust gases. We could go to the moon in one trip, to Mars and Venus with only an orbital refueling. The space station was obsolete and unnecessary before it was a third finished and we landed on the moon five years ahead of schedule.

"Oh, we finished the space station, but on a smaller scale than planned, and mostly just as an observation station for the meteorologists. And we put the second one, the twenty-four hour one, up there just for telecasting. And meanwhile—"

"Max, I've read rocket history. You're telling me your own experiences and background, remember?"

"Oh, sure. Well, suddenly I wasn't so far down the line. The atomic rockets were being built in quantity. They really worked, and thirty of them were finished in sixty-five, forty more in sixty-six, and they were getting into the four-man jobs by then and so I was in. I got to the moon in late sixty-six, co-pilot and navigator on a two-man rocket with a five-ton pay load for the observatory that we were starting to build there. Co-piloted once more, to Mars in the next year, and then I was made spaceman first class and full pilot. I was twenty-six, but they'd extended active duty age to thirty, where it is now, so I still had four years ahead of me.

"But damn it, I got retired at twenty-seven just the same. An accident on a routine surface exploration trip to Venus—the eighth trip we'd made there; I never got a first."

"What kind of an accident, Max?"

"We'd finished our mission; we were checking the rocket for take-off. I was outside, climbing up to check the solars, but the co-pilot thought I was inside and fired a short test burst from the steering jets. I had a leg in front of one of them and that was the end of that leg, from just below the knee. They got me back to Earth alive and I lived, but that was the end of my being a spaceman."

She said, "Oh," quietly, and then, "I'm sorry, Max."

"I'm not," I said. "I mean, I wouldn't have the leg back at the expense of not having made the six trips I made into space. A lot of the early spacemen paid with their lives for one trip. I was lucky. Six trips for only a leg."

"Yes, you'd feel that way. Go on."

"Go on where? That's all."

She laughed a little. "You were only twenty-seven then and you're fifty-seven now. What happened to you in between?"

"I made myself a rocket mech. I could have had a pension but turned it down in favor of their giving me all the courses they had in atomics and rocket mech work. And I've been a rocket mech ever since. That's all."

I thought a moment. "No, by God, that isn't all. If I'm trying to give you the full picture I've got no business being modest. I made myself into a *good* rocket mech, one of the best in the country. And I've kept abreast of improvements in them; I know them inside out and I can fix anything that ever went wrong with one. I'm not a nuclear physicist as far as theory goes but I've got a thorough working knowledge of applied atomics. I know and have worked on commercial passenger rockets, mail rockets and interplanetaries.

"I haven't worked on the interplanetaries since I passed the government's age limit for mechs seven years ago, but I've kept up with every change that's been made in them—and I've even had a few minor suggestions of my own for improvements accepted and used."

I said, "This will sound like I'm bragging, but I've worked at every one of the twelve commercial rocket ports in this country and I can work at any one of them again any time I want to, starting at one minute's notice and whether they're short of men or not. And even though I'll never ride a rocket again, I've kept up on every new technique in astrogation that's been tried out or used. I'm a fair amateur astronomer, and not just the star-gazing kind that can tell one celestial object from another. I can calculate orbits and trajectories and eclipses."

"Do you have an engineering degree?"

"No, just a bachelor of science degree—that came with graduation from space school in those days, and don't think we didn't earn it. But as far as knowledge goes, I'm a rocket engineer. Might have to bone up on a few points to get an engineering degree, but I could get one. I just never bothered because I like mech work better. I like to work on rockets themselves, not on pictures of rockets on paper."

"You've never done administrative work, then?"

"No. I don't like it."

"But would you do it on Project Jupiter?"

"I'll sweep floors if I have to get on. But I'd rather be head mech."

"Would you like to be assistant director?"

I took a deep breath. I said, "Yes."

"Max, I may be able to swing it for you—on a couple of conditions. And it would mean you'd really be running the project. The project director will have to be a political figure; there's no out on that. But the assistant director won't have to be, and he'll be the one who runs things—with the director as a figurehead. Would you like that, Max? To run the project and build and send the rocket?"

"Woman, don't ask crazy questions. And the two conditions are granted. What are they?"

"You're not going to like them," she said. "And I'm not going to tell you now, because it might lead to argument."

"It won't," I said. "I'll agree to anything, even cutting off my other leg. Or my head, for that matter."

"You'll need your head. And as for cutting off your other leg, this may hurt worse. But Max, we've talked pretty long and I'm getting tired. Want to come back again tomorrow evening, same time?"

I wanted to.

Back home I started to do some grinding on the reflector

for my telescope, but grinding is painstaking and ticklish work so I quit when I found that my hands were trembling.

Not that I could blame them for trembling. They had a chance now, an outside chance, a thousand-to-one-against chance, of going to Jupiter, of piloting a rocket that was going out into space eight times as far as Mars, eight times as far into space as a rocket had ever been before.

A chance in a thousand. But yesterday it had been a chance in a million. A few months ago a chance in a billion, or no chance at all.

No, I didn't blame my hands for trembling.

§

"The conditions?" I asked Ellen Gallagher.

"Let's have the amenities first. May I offer you a drink, Max, to fortify you?"

"The conditions, woman. Quit stalling."

"First, a degree in rocket engineering. You said you could get one if you wanted it. Can you get one before the project appointments are made? Say within a year?"

I groaned. "I can, but it will mean some tough slogging. I'll have to pass examinations in about ten subjects. Six of them I can pass as of right now, but four will take me some pretty heavy studying. They're things I know from the practical side, but I'm going to have to absorb some theory. Yes, I can do it in a year. Maybe less. And what's the other condition?"

"That you get into administrative work, now. And between now and the time the appointments are made work yourself up to as high a spot as you can."

I groaned again.

She said, "Here's why, Max. The project will be set up so the project director appoints his own assistant—but it will have to be subject to presidential approval; you'll have to look good to pass that."

I said, "But if the President appoints the director, how'll you swing any weight as to who the director makes his assistant?"

She smiled. "Because it will be a deal. I'll pick my figure-head for director—someone with a big name but out of a job and looking for one—and I'll offer to recommend him for the job on the condition that he appoint you his assistant. If he wants the directorship badly enough, he'll agree —up to a point. But I still won't be able to sell him a simple, barefoot rocket mech, Max. You can see that."

"I'm afraid I can. How high will I have to get?"

"The higher the better. But any responsible administrative job with a big rocket port ought to do it. That and your being an accredited rocket engineer. Not to mention the glamour of your being an ex-spaceman."

"And if I go through all that and then the President does his own picking out of a project director?"

"A chance you take. But I think I can make my recommendation stick—by the simple expedient of picking a man who'll be completely acceptable to the President, whom he might pick anyway if I didn't make a recommendation. And there are other angles. Complicated to explain—but I'm pretty sure I can swing it. If you can get that degree

63

and get yourself into a job with a good sounding title. Can you?"

"I can," I said. "I fear that I can. Any other conditions?"

"No."

"Then I'll have that drink you offered me. I need it. Where is it?"

"In that cabinet in the corner. Make anything you want and please pour me a glass of the sherry."

I took sherry too. I had some heavy thinking coming up.

I said, "Los Angeles Rocket Port is my best bet. It's one of the biggest, for one thing. For another, the superintendent there is a friend of mine, the closest friend I've got among the brass. He came up from being a mech himself and we talk the same language.

"And he's been heckling me for years to wash the grease off my hands and get into the office end. He'll start me in as a department head if there's an opening. If there isn't, he'll give me the best thing open and swing me up as fast as he can. I might, with luck, even get to be assistant superintendent within a year. In fact—"

I thought a minute. "In fact, if we want to be Machiavellian about it, and why shouldn't we, I can tell him the score and why I need the title for a front. And he can probably fix it for me to be holding the title temporarily just while the appointments to Project Jupiter are being made. Hell yes, he'll do that for me. And by then I can have saved up enough so we can give his regular assistant a month or so off with my paying his salary for the period I hold his job for a front. Sure Klockerman will do that."

"Assistant superintendent would be fine. Even your being a department head might be enough. How soon can you start?"

"A day or two, I guess. Luckily we're slack on work at Treasure so I won't be leaving Rory in a jam—and even if I was, he'd understand when I tell him the score. Sure, I can leave here tomorrow. I'll call up Klockerman tonight after I get home and talk to him. And I'll see Rory tonight and catch the first jet out."

She laughed a little. "The thing I like about you, Max, is that you don't do things by halves. Returning favors aside, I really want you to run Project Jupiter. You'll do a good job of it."

"I'll do my best," I said. "Damn you, Senator, I ought to hate you for making the next year of my life the miserable one it's going to be, but I love you instead. How soon are you going to be well enough for me to make a pass at you?"

She laughed again. "You'd do even that for a chance to run the project?"

"I'd do even that," I said. "But we'll postpone discussion of it now. And let's consider my plans settled and quit talking about me. Tell me something about the project, about the rocket itself. Bradly had it all figured out?"

"To the last decimal, Max. A detailed prospectus. But the prospectus is in my safe in Los Angeles and you can see it after I go back home there. I could tell you a few things about it, but I've no head for technical details and I might get some of them wrong. You might as well wait till you can read the prospectus and get the whole thing at once."

"All right," I said. "How soon will you be in L. A.?"

"Within a month if I keep on improving as fast as I have, and with no setbacks. About the first of March, maybe. As soon as you're settled there, write me so I'll have your address and phone and can let you know when I'm coming."

"Fine," I said. "Will do. But won't you tell me even a few simple things about the rocket now, so I can be thinking about them?"

"Please don't ask me to, Max. I'm getting tired now and you've stayed pretty long. If we get started talking about the rocket now it'll be hard to stop. And everything about it is in Brad's prospectus that you'll be seeing. It was Brad's baby."

It was Brad's baby, and she was carrying it. I wondered if that meant anything and decided it was none of my business if it did. I'd just been kidding about making that pass. Or had I been kidding? She was a damned attractive woman.

I went straight to Rory's instead of back to my room, and as soon as I'd told Rory the score I phoned Klockerman. It was okay. He wanted me. Best he could do right off was to give me charge of the tool room but he had a couple of department heads who weren't too satisfactory and he thought that within a month at the outside he could move me up. I didn't, over the phone, tell him my real reason for switching from mech work or how high and fast I wanted to rise. Time enough for that later, over a drink or two.

I offered Rory the optical blanks I'd started to grind; it takes a lot of evenings to grind a good reflector for a scope and my evenings were going to be busy for a long time. I still wanted a scope to look at Jupiter with but now I'd have to buy one instead of making it. Rory wanted the blanks and drove me to my room so he could pick them up. He waited while I packed and then took me to the square where I could catch a helicab to the stratojet field on Angel. I was in Los Angeles by midnight.

§

February, March I worked days, studied nights.

But I was making progress both ways. At the rocket port I was head of a department, maintenance. Dull stuff, but it gave me a title. And I gave it all I had and was doing well; it looked like I might get that first assistantship honestly, without finagling, and within the year. I hadn't leveled with Klockerman yet; I'd decided that if I could get as far as that assistantship on my own, finagling might get me even farther. If I got to be his assistant honestly, before I told Klocky what I was really working for, then he might let me pull a real coup by taking a month or so off at the crucial time and leaving me as acting superintendent of the third largest rocket port in the world.

On the scholastic front I was down to four subjects, the four tough ones. I'd learned there were only nine subjects I'd have to pass examinations in to get that engineering degree and three of them were so easy I didn't even need refreshing in them. I got those three out of the way the first week. A week's study took care of the next two. Of the four I had left, two were subjects I knew but hadn't used for so long I was pretty rusty in them. But I could bone up on them myself and take the exams within another month.

That would get me down to the two, the ones that were going to be toughies for me. Extreme-temperature metallurgy and unified field theory. Neither of them are things I'd ever figured a rocket engineer needed to know. You can take the characteristics of all metals and all common alloys from charts that have been worked out to the tenth decimal; what's the advantage of being able to calculate them yourself? Unified field theory is even worse; nobody yet has worked out a unified field theory that's *more* than a theory or has any practical application to rocket engineering. Besides, it's got to be approached through relativity, and relativity sets my teeth on edge because it tries to set limits; I don't believe in limits.

Yes, when I got to those two subjects I'd need tutoring, but there are plenty of Caltech instructors and even professors willing to pick up some money on the side by giving the kind of help I'd need, and with a good salary coming in and no free time to spend any of it, I had money to burn.

§

Senator Gallagher returned in early April. I met her at the jetport but there were others meeting her too and I didn't join the entourage that escorted her home; I just managed to talk to her long enough to make an appointment for the first evening she had free. She seemed to be almost completely recovered and told me she expected to go to Washington within another month to take her place in the Senate for the final month or so of the current session.

My appointment was for two evenings later and she promised to hold the whole evening for me so we'd have time to go over the prospectus for the rocket.

§

"Drink, Max?"

"Woman," I said. "Show me that prospectus. I've been waiting months now to see it."

Ellen shook her head wonderingly. "Even administrative work doesn't civilize you, Max. You're a savage. And you have a strictly one-track mind."

"Exactly," I told her. "And it's on the prospectus. Let's see it."

"Not until we've had a drink and a minimum of fifteen minutes of civilized conversation. You've waited months and a few more minutes won't kill you."

I made us drinks. And I made myself be polite and patient, even beyond the time she'd set. I waited twenty-two minutes before I again asked to see the prospectus.

She brought it to me.

I took a quick glance at the sketch of the rocket and I screamed. Not aloud, but inside my mind. I leafed over to the recapitulation of the costs and wanted to tear my hair out by the roots.

My face must have shown how I felt. Ellen asked, "What's wrong, Max?"

"A step-rocket!" I said. "Shades of nineteen sixty-two, a step-rocket! Ellen, it doesn't take a step-rocket to go to Jupiter, not with atomics! And the cost—three hundred and ten million! I can send a rocket to Jupiter and back for a tenth that much. Fifty million at the very most. This is crazy."

"Are you sure, Max? Brad was a rocket engineer, too—and one of the top ones."

"Sure, but—wait, give me a few minutes to skim through this to see where he went off the beam."

I skimmed, and shuddered.

I said, "Point one. He's using a two-man rocket. Why? One man's plenty. One man can do all the necessary recording and observing and have time on his hands to boot, even while he's rounding Jupe."

"Brad and I talked about that. He said that an entire year alone in space is too much for any—"

"Nuts," I said. "The first trip to Mars, circle and return without landing, was made by Ortman in sixty-five and he was alone in space four hundred and twenty-two days. The living compartment in that rocket was three feet in diameter by six and a half feet long, just a good roomy coffin. And there wasn't a cadet in space school who didn't envy him every minute of that trip.

"Woman, this trip to Jupiter is another *first*, and the first in more years than any spaceman likes to think about.

A thousand qualified men will be fighting for the privilege of making that trip, no matter what the conditions are, no matter how tough it's going to be."

I looked at the prospectus again. "A ten-foot-diameter living compartment, that's what Brad figured here. Now even if it had to be a two-man rocket, which it doesn't, that's silly for a *first*. He picked that because it's standard on a two-man Mars rocket, but Mars is a milk run. One man, a four-foot-diameter compartment, that's plenty. That's luxury. And it cuts down the weight of that part of the rocket by about 70 per cent."

Ellen shuddered. "I know I'd hate to spend a year in a space that size."

"Sure, but you're not a spaceman. Spacemen are tough, mentally and physically. They've got to be to get *into* space school, let alone get through it and graduate.

"And one of the first things they psych them for, Ellen, is claustrophobia. And if they've got the faintest touch of it they're out unless it can be completely cured. They're trained to be alone with themselves for long periods when necessary. Why, with the psychoanalysis they put them through today a trip like that one is a breeze."

I grinned. "Ellen, when I entered space school back when, psychoanalysis wasn't what it is today. Know how they tested us for claustrophobia, our first week in? Each of us would be locked up in a dark closet exactly two feet square—you couldn't even sit down in it—and each of us had to stay in one of those closets forty-eight hours, and stay awake. There was a button he had to press every hour on the hour—he had a watch with a radium dial so

71

he'd know the time—to prove that he was awake and okay. Or if a guy felt himself getting scared or starting to go crazy, he could give three quick rings on the same button and they'd come and let him out—out of the closet and the school both. That was just *one* of the cute little mental and physical endurance tests we had to go through in those days, and not the worst one by a long shot."

"But Max, Brad *did* try figuring a one-man rocket, and he said it would have to be a step-rocket anyway so the cost would be only slightly more to make it a two-man ship so—"

"Quiet," I said. "I'm reading some more of this horrible document. Aha—here's the big joker, Ellen. Here's why he thought he'd need a step-rocket even for a one-man ship; he's figuring on carrying the eagle for the whole trip, the round trip!

"The eagle?"

"Slang for E. G. L., exhaust gas liquid. You see Ellen, an atomic rocket doesn't have to carry fuel—unless you count the consumption inside the micropile and that's negligible weight-wise—in the same sense that an old-type chemical rocket had to carry fuel. But an atomic rocket has to carry tanks of some liquid for the heat pile to turn into gases, the gases that come out of the exhaust vents and drive the rocket."

"I understand that. But why *doesn't* the rocket have to carry exhaust gas liquid for the whole trip? It's a circle trip."

I was pacing the floor with that damned prospectus in my hand. I said, "Sure, it's a circle trip as far as Jupiter is concerned. But Jupiter's got twelve moons, any one of them easy to land on and take off from because of low gravity. And at least seven of them lousy with frozen ammonia. For free, all you want."

"But would ammonia work?"

"Any reasonably inert liquid works. Ammonia works fine. It's been tried, on the test block. The only strike against it is that at ordinary temperatures, it's a gas unless it's kept under pressure in the tank. A pressurized tank has to be a heavier tank; it adds to the weight of the rocket and so cuts down the pay load."

"But in that case, Max—"

"The difference in rocket weight, though, in using pressurized tanks is slight, almost negligible, compared to the weight difference of having to carry exhaust gas liquid for the round trip. That's big enough to make the difference between a one-stage rocket and a three-stage. Between fifty million and three hundred million."

Ellen leaned forward. "Max, that would make a tremendous difference. If it can be done as cheaply as that— Are you *sure?*"

I said, "I'll make sure. Right now. I'll be back tomorrow evening. Same time." I stood up.

"Don't rush off—"

I rushed off. Home. Limbered up my slide rule on a few preliminaries and then realized I didn't have all the data I'd need to work it out thoroughly. Klockerman would have it all, either in his head or his library. And he'd be better than I, particularly in figuring costs; that was where I'd be weakest.

I called him and explained, told him we'd better work at his place because all the data would be there. I called a helicab.

We worked all night.

We figured it. Not exactly, but to one decimal place, near enough to show that it would work, and easily. And I'd guessed high on the cost. Klocky figured it to be twenty-six million, less than a tenth the cost of Bradly's step-rocket.

We topped the coffee we'd been drinking all night with breakfast and benzedrine and went to work.

That night I gave the results to Ellen. She studied them wonderingly. Especially the table of costs and its total.

"You say Klockerman worked with you on this?"

"It's more his work than mine."

"He's good, isn't he?"

"The best," I said. "The best, that is, outside of a few boys in government service, at Los Alamos and White Sands. And of course they'll go over those specifications later, before the rocket's actually started. But I'll guarantee you, Ellen, they'll find nothing fundamentally wrong. They may make minor changes, may insist on upping a few safety factors slightly, but they won't up the estimate more than 10 per cent at the very most, and that's still under thirty million."

She nodded slowly. "Then this is the rocket we'll use. Now, Max, make us a drink and we'll drink to it."

We drank to it. I gave us each a straight drink first that we could down as a toast, and then I made a pair of high-balls for leisurely sipping.

Ellen sipped hers thoughtfully. "Max, this is going to

74

change things a lot. It gives me an idea. I'm going to Washington in two weeks. I'm well now, but I'm going to take two more weeks for a little more rest and some planning. And do you know what I'm going to do as soon as I get to the Senate?"

"Sure. Since this is only a tenth what you thought you'd have to ask for, you'll try to get it through this session. Right?"

"Wrong. This year it would be vetoed regardless of amount and even if I could get it through that quickly, and I couldn't. No, I've got an idea that will get this through like a shot next session, early next session. As soon as I get to Washington I'm going to put an appropriation bill in the hopper based on Brad's step-rocket."

"My God," I yelled. "Why?"

"Quiet." She grinned. "Yes, the three hundred ten million dollar rocket. But I'll also make sure that it stays in committee and doesn't get voted on. Early next session, the first week, I go to the committee and offer to withdraw that bill in favor of a substitute one—one-tenth the size. Max, I'll have it through both houses and past the President in a month!"

I said, "Senator, I love you."

She laughed. "It's the rocket you love. The rocket and Jupiter."

"And the stars. But you too, Senator Ellen Gallagher."

Suddenly it came to me that I'd *meant* what I'd just said.

I loved her, and because she was a woman, not because she was pushing a rocket.

I went over and sat beside her on the sofa, put my arm

around her and kissed her. And again, and this time her arms came up around me, pulling me to her tightly.

"You damned fool," she said, "why did you wait so long to do that?"

§

I decided that a couple of weeks off studying would do me more good than harm in the long run. I was ahead of schedule on my studies and I was pretty sure that I'd get the degree in plenty of time; a little rest would keep me from getting stale.

So I spent most of my evenings those two weeks with Ellen. A few nights too, but we were discreet about it. A scandal wouldn't have helped Ellen's career.

And marriage was definitely out of the question, if for no other reason than that it would have kept me off the Jupiter project. Nepotism had become a nasty word in government by the nineties; the old days when congressmen got their relatives on government payrolls, even in minor capacities, were gone. With Ellen sponsoring the Jupiter project she couldn't possibly have sponsored a husband for a job on it.

Klockerman knew about Ellen and me, but he was one of the family by then. We'd even leveled with him about my real reason for taking an administrative job under him, and he'd told me that he'd guarantee my being acting superintendent of the port at the time the project appointments came up, that he'd take as much time off as necessary, even six months, and leave me in charge. He said he was due for a long vacation anyhow and that there were places he wanted to see and things he wanted to do.

Life was suddenly being very good to an aging ex-spaceman. I was happier than I'd been for more years than I liked to think about.

§

Ellen went to Washington the third week in April. She'd be gone at least a month, possibly as long as two, depending on how long Congress stayed in session.

I missed her like hell. Funny how quickly you can get used to a woman. Here I'd hardly thought about one for several years, and now after only two weeks of Ellen there was a big hole in my life when she went away, even though she'd be back soon.

Back to my studies. The rest from them had sharpened my mind and had done me good. Two weeks saw me through the two subjects I'd been refreshing myself in, both those examinations out of the way. Down to the two toughies. I found myself a Caltech boy who knew extreme-temperature metallurgy and with him tutoring me four evenings a week, I dived in. Two other evenings a week I'd study alone. One evening a week, usually Sunday, I spent at Klocky's place, playing chess, drinking a little beer, talking.

On the study nights, either alone or after my tutor had left, I'd read until my eyes would start to blur. Then I'd quit and if it was a clear night with good seeing I'd go up on the roof and rest my eyes by looking far with them for a while, through the telescope I'd bought myself and had mounted up there.

Jupiter was nearing opposition, coming almost as close to Earth as he ever gets. Only four hundred million miles away he'd be in another few weeks, not much more than that now. Big Jupiter, the giant of the solar system, eleven times as big as Earth in diameter, three hundred times as great in mass. More than twice as big as all the other planets in the system put together.

Big Jupiter with its twelve moons. Four of them visible through my telescope. The others all tiny, a hundred miles or less in diameter. It takes a big scope to find them.

But four of them I could see, the four that are as big as Earth's moon or bigger, the four that Galileo had discovered in 1610, with the first crude telescope he made.

Four moons, four cold but lovely moons which man had never reached but which man was going to reach and set foot upon. Soon. Damned soon.

Io. Europa. Ganymede. Callisto.

Which would I land upon? Or would I ever land on any? Max, I told myself, Max you silly fool you dreamer, it's still a thousand to one chance. The rocket is going, yes, the rocket will be built and you'll supervise the building of it. But Max you ass, your chance of stealing it? It's going to be a government project with guards, with hundreds of people working on it. Sure, you can arrange *some* of the things you'll have to arrange; you can have it fueled and loaded and ready to take off twenty-four or forty-eight hours before actual take-off time; you can arrange some-how to have the orbital refueling rocket up there already, ahead of time—yes, you can give reasons for that; you can finagle something that will get the director himself off the grounds so you'll be in full charge at the crucial time. But still so many things could go wrong, so many things. . . .

Still a chance in a thousand. But a chance to go on eight times as far as Mars, ten times as far out into space as man had ever been before.

A little closer to the stars, the far far stars that someday we're going to reach, the billion billion billion stars that are waiting for us.

§

Ellen came back in the middle of July.

We saw one another, of course, the night she got back, but then not again for a week. I was so close to being ready for my exam in metallurgy that we agreed not to see one another again until I had it over with. That gave me a double incentive to burn midnight oil and I really burned it. The seeing was bad that week, too, so I wasn't even tempted to the roof, and I skipped my usual evening with Klocky.

So it was just seven days on the head after Ellen's return that I was able to phone Ellen that I'd passed my second last exam and had only one subject left between me and the degree.

"Wonderful, darling," she said. "And you're not going

to start the last subject right away, are you? You're way ahead of schedule."

"Right, Ellen. And here's another item of good news. Klocky has been more than satisfied with the way I'm handling the maintenance department. Says he'll use my getting that degree as occasion for making me assistant supervisor. That'll give me at least several months of experience before he takes off for a while and leaves me as acting super."

"Max, things are really working out. Just as they are in Washington. Coming over tonight to celebrate?"

"Is that a new word for it?"

"Don't be vulgar, darling. I've got some champagne. Does that tempt you?"

"It would, except that I've got a better idea. I can take a week off at the rocket port, starting as of now. What are your plans?"

"Why—I have a few appointments, one viddy appearance, a meeting or two—"

"Could you cancel them? We could run down to Mexico City for a week. We can be there in time for dinner this evening."

We went down to Mexico City for a week.

It was a wonderful week, and also a restful one. We were both tired and got plenty of sleep, slept till noon every day and sometimes even later. Evenings, but never into the small hours of the night, we saw the sights and went the round of the bright spots. Ellen wore a skin mask, of course —one of the new Ravigos that can hardly be detected even

80

in daylight—whenever we were outside our suite. The price of being famous.

I really got to know Senator Ellen Gallagher that week. She told me just about everything important that had ever happened to her.

She'd had a kind of rough early life. She'd been born Ellen Grabow, and she'd never seen her father; he'd been a casualty in fifty-two in that mess we were embroiled in then in Korea, just a few weeks before she was born. Her mother had died two years later; the grandparents on her father's side had tried to take care of her but they were too poor to have a nurse or governess, too old and one of them too ill to raise her themselves. They'd had to put her in an orphanage.

She'd been an ugly duckling, a sickly, unattractive child with chronic skin trouble and frequent colds. Also, she admitted, pretty much of an unmanageable brat because of her dissatisfaction with herself and her overcompensations for her feelings of inferiority. She'd been adopted on a trial basis three times between the ages of three and eight and turned back to the orphanage at the end of the trial period or before.

The fourth offer, when she was ten, she effectively turned down herself with a tantrum that frightened off the prospective adopters. She stayed at the orphanage until she was fifteen; she was then released—on parole, as it were—to take a job, on the conditions that she must live at a girls' club until she was of age and that she must continue her studies at night school until she had a high school diploma. Her job was in the package room of a department store and she stuck at it two weeks until she got her first pay check. All of this had been in Wichita, Kansas.

She so thoroughly hated Wichita and the conditions of her parole that she used that first money she got to jump parole and take a bus to Hollywood. She was enamoured of acting and wanted to get into the booming viddy field. (That was the year they'd built the second space station, the telestation for viddy only, and it had gone up right over her head in Kansas.) She was still unattractive at fifteen and knew it, but thought she had great acting ability and that she could do character parts and brat roles, possibly even become a comedienne.

Perhaps, she admitted, thinking of herself as being funny or potentially funny had been her defense against her own unattractiveness during adolescence. Instead of admiring herself in her mirror, she used to practice making funny faces at her self.

§

"Intermission," I said.

I got up and made us each a drink, brought them back to bed. Ellen had propped up pillows for us and we lay back against them. We sipped our drinks.

"Have I been boring you, Max?" she asked.

"You never have and you never will," I told her. "Go on."

§

82

She went on. She went on, to California and to what she hoped would be sudden success in the viddies.

But two years in Hollywood, working as a waitress, convinced her that she wasn't going to get a chance to try; then she did get a couple of chances and failed to get either part or any encouragement whatsoever, and that convinced her she'd better start looking for something more likely than a viddy career.

Something more likely turned out to be Ray Connor, a young man only a year older than she, who wanted to marry her. At eighteen he was an orphan too, but a recent one who had a little money and a small income from his parents' estate. He wanted to become a lawyer and a statesman, and he was just starting to put himself through law school. When they were married he suggested that she enter college too and was a little horrified to learn that she was a year and a half short of having finished high school. Ellen was beginning by then to be aware of the shortcomings of her education and readily agreed to study high school subjects at home, with her husband's help, until she could take college entrance examinations.

She was surprised to find that she enjoyed studying and learning, now that she was doing it because she wanted to and not because she had to. She made the college examinations in only six months—sooner than she'd have gotten a diploma if she'd stayed in Wichita and had continued going to night school there. She entered college only a term behind her husband and she too decided to study law. She'd become interested in it through his interest and had begun to see herself as a Portia, perhaps even as a stateswoman; that was in the early seventies when women were going more and more into politics.

She made up the term she was behind Ray and they graduated together in seventy-five; she was twenty-three then and he was twenty-four. And it was right in the middle of the Depression and there were no jobs or partnerships for young and inexperienced lawyers; even the older ones were barely hanging on, like people in every other profession except psychiatry. And Ray's money was gone. They had to look for any kind of work they could get, just to keep eating. Ellen was the first to get a job because of her experience as a waitress and the comparatively rapid turnover in waitress work even in depression times. It took Ray three months of hunting before he got any kind of work at all. It was a construction job. On his third day at it he fell from a girder four stories in the air and was killed.

§

"Did you love him, Ellen?" I asked.

"Yes, by then, very much. I'm afraid I married him mostly for practical reasons, but in five years I'd come to love him very deeply."

"Have you loved many men, Ellen?"

"Four, only four. Three besides you."

§

Ralph Gallagher was the second.

She met him four years later when she was a law clerk in the firm of Gallagher, Reyoll and Wilcox. He was older than she, but not too much older, forty-one to her twenty-seven. He was already becoming prominent in politics and was well on his way to being a big man. He'd been married once but had been divorced several years.

Ellen had admired him, looked up to him. When, several months after she started to work there, he began to notice her and be friendly to her, she was pleased. When he'd taken her out a few times, she was even more pleased to learn that he was looking for a wife and not a mistress, and that he thought she would be just right for the job.

She married him. And for the ten years they had together before his death she merged her own ambitions with his; she made being his wife her career. She learned how to entertain for him. She learned politics, the practical kind, and used them to help him. She helped make him mayor of Los Angeles and an almost certain winner in the next election for the governorship of California.

But coronary thrombosis got him first.

And Ellen got another shock. She was broke again, flat broke. Familiar as she had been with his political affairs she had paid no attention to his financial ones, and he had stupidly put all his eggs into one basket, a basket with no bottom in it. His estate, after final expenses were paid out of it, was barely going to break even.

Ellen had had a law education but had never practiced; it would have been late for her to start at thirty-seven.

But she knew politics and she bore a name that was respected in California, especially in Los Angeles.

She ran for city council and won easily, won a second time by an even bigger vote two years later, was made president of the council. Then two terms in the state assembly. And after that she was talked by the leaders of her party into running in the special election to fill the unexpired portion of the Senate term of a man who had died in office.

§

"And would have been miserably defeated, Max, if you hadn't pulled a rabbit out of a hat."

"Out of your opponent's office, my love. But you skipped over man-I-love number three. Was it Bradly?"

"Yes, it was Brad. For about a year, a couple of years ago. It ended then, sort of by mutual consent and without even a quarrel, so I guess it couldn't have been too serious."

"But he came to you with the Jupiter project? Or had he sold you on that before?"

"A little of both. He'd talked about it before, while we were in love or thought we were, but just in a general way. When he heard I was running for the Senate he came to me with the specific plans, the prospectus, and asked me to try to get it through if I won. I told him I would, never dreaming he'd make the political mistake of talking about it to reporters just before the election. If I'd foreseen that, I'd never have agreed."

I said, "You don't mean that. You mean you'd have warned him to keep his yap shut. Or—do you mean you weren't really enthusiastic about the project itself? That it was just your friendship with Bradly that made you agree?"

"Well, it was partly that. Oh, I liked the idea of a rocket going out to Jupiter. I wanted to see man take another step out, in my lifetime. But it wasn't really important to me and I certainly wouldn't have staked my political career on it. You want to know, Max, when I got really enthusiastic about that rocket? The evening I first met you. The look in your eyes, the way you talked, the way you thought. I guess a little stardust rubbed off on me that evening. I found myself talking about horse trading that bill through Congress as though it was the most important legislation in the world—and suddenly it was."

"And did you know that evening what was going to happen between us?"

"Of course. Almost as soon as you walked in the doorway."

I shook my head wonderingly. "Would you like a drink?" I asked her.

She would. I got up and made one for each of us.

Back in bed, sitting up with drinks in our hands, we talked some more.

"Max, do you *really* think we'll ever reach the stars? They're light years away, and a light-year is a frightening distance."

"It is, if you let it frighten you."

"How far is the nearest one? I've heard, but I've forgotten."

"Proxima Centauri is about four light years. And we still don't know how far the farthest ones are because the galaxies keep on going for all the billions of light years our telescopes show us. Maybe the relativists' finite universe is wrong and they go on forever. Maybe there *is* an infinity."

"And an eternity?"

"You're in the middle of that now. This talk about the age of the universe being a specific figure—two billion years, four billion years—nuts. Can you think that suddenly somebody or something wound up a clock and started it running, that there wasn't any *time* before a certain specific moment? Time can't be stopped or started, damn it. If this particular universe does have a definite age, isn't eternal and constantly renewing itself by some process we don't yet understand, then there must have been universes before this one. In eternity there could be an infinite progression of universes, an infinite number of them past and an infinite number to come.

"Maybe, Ellen, there was a universe umpteen billion years ago in which two people were sitting up beside one another in bed, just as we are, with maybe the same names we have, drinking the same drinks, saying the same things —except that maybe they were wearing different colored pajamas because that was a different universe."

Ellen laughed. "But half an hour before, then, they weren't wearing any pajamas at all so you couldn't have told the difference. But Max, leaving time and eternity out of it, do you really believe the relativists are wrong about the universe being finite in volume, space curving

88

back on itself? Even finite, they allow for it being pretty big, you know."

I took a sip of my drink. I said, "I hope they're wrong, because no matter how big they decide it is, if it's finite then there must be a farthest star, and I don't like to think there is. Where would we go from there?"

"But if space curves on itself, wouldn't the farthest star be the nearest one too?"

"Woman," I said, "that is *really* a frightening thought. It makes me dizzy. I refuse to buy it, or even examine it. Let's get back to a finite universe. If this one is finite, there could still be an infinite number of universes like it, an infinity of finites. Like drops of water. Maybe we are like animalculae in a drop of water that happens to be separate from other drops of water, a universe in itself. Do you suppose the animalculae ever suspect that there are other drops of water besides theirs?"

"One of them might. *You* just did. But Max, what if *our* drop of water is on the slide of a microscope or some equivalent of a microscope and what if Something is looking at us right now?"

"Let it look," I said. "As long as it behaves itself. And if it doesn't, I'll slap it down."

§

Back to Los Angeles, back to maintenance, back to study. Not quite so strict a regime this time, now that I was down to one subject, with the degree in sight. Ellen convinced me that all work and no play would make me a dull boy and I didn't want to be a dull boy. I studied four evenings a week, two of them solo and two of them with coaching. Two evenings a week I saw Ellen or Klocky or both of them, one evening I just read and rested. Usually my evenings with Ellen were quiet ones at her apartment but occasionally we took in a show or a concert. It didn't matter if we were seen together once in a while as long as we avoided the plush places frequented by the gossip columnists and commentators; we didn't want our names coupled in print or on the viddy because even a suggestion of romance between us would be bad when the time came for Ellen to use pressure to get me on the project.

July, August, September.

I was making a new friend, too, in the man who was coaching me in unified field theory. His name was improbable, Chang M'bassi, but he himself was much more improbable than his name.

Chang M'bassi was the last, or believed to be the last, of the Masai tribesmen who, until the late sixties, had lived in east equatorial Africa. They don't live there any more because they're all dead except M'bassi; at least there is no other authenticated case of a survivor among them. They were perhaps the most colorful of all the African tribes and the fiercest and bravest warriors. They were the tall ones, averaging well over six feet in height. Their sport was hunting lions with spears; no youth became a full member of the tribe until he had killed his lion. They did not hunt other game and seldom ate meat; they were herders as well as warriors. They had great herds of cattle

90

and their staple diet, almost the only food they ate, was a mixture of milk and cattle blood. That diet proved fatal to them in the great plague, the sudden disaster that struck equatorial Africa in, if I have the year right, 1969, killing fifteen or sixteen million people within a few weeks. The plague came the year following the first large-scale attempt to exterminate the tsetse fly in that area. The attempt was almost but not completely successful; a few of the tsetses proved immune or developed immunity to the new "wondercide" that was being used against them. They came back the next year greatly diminished in number but they had in them a new or hitherto unknown virus with which they infected cattle, and a strange triple-play death struck the region. The cattle showed no outward signs of illness from the infection, nor did human beings who were infected directly by the tsetse flies. But in the blood and in the milk of infected cattle the virus underwent a change that made it deadly to humans. Eating meat, blood or milk from an infected cow was fatal. Vomiting started in hours, helplessness within a day, death within three to four days.

When the plague struck, less than a week after the tsetses had swarmed in from their breeding places, the Masai hadn't had a chance. They'd all been infected, almost simultaneously; all of them, except a boy named M'bassi, were ill before the epidemologists could get there, all of them except M'bassi were dead before an effective treatment could be found. The epidemologists had quickly isolated the virus and its source and had immediately spread the warning to avoid beef and milk. Because of these warnings and because within a week the epidemologists had found an effective treatment for the disease itself, no other tribes had casualties higher than half their numbers. Not even those tribes who were also primarily herdsmen; their herds had not been as quickly and as thoroughly infected as those of the Masai.

M'bassi's survival had been accidental or providential, whichever way you want to look at it. A Chinese medical missionary, one Chang Wo Sing, a Buddhist, had just arrived among them to try to convert them to the Eightfold Path. He would have had a tough job doing it because his particular sect of Buddhism, besides being evangelical, preached rigid vegetarianism and was against the killing of animals. To embrace the philosophy he brought to them, the Masai—well, it's anybody's guess now whether they would have been more horrified at the thought of eating vegetables or the thought of giving up their passionate devotion for hunting lions. He might have had more luck making non-violent vegetarians out of the lions.

But in a limited way—limited to one person—Chang Wo Sing had actually succeeded in converting the entire Masai people to his way of thinking. M'bassi, last of the Masai, was a Buddhist.

M'bassi had been eleven years old then, a son of the chief of the particular Masai village upon which Dr. Chang had benevolently descended. And on the very day of the good doctor's arrival there M'bassi had been badly mauled by a lion about half a mile outside the village. He had been brought in mercifully unconscious but more nearly dead than alive, with very little blood left in him. His father the

92

chief, no doubt giving the boy up for dead in any case, had shown no hesitancy in letting the Chinaman try to save his life.

Dr. Chang had tried and succeeded. But M'bassi a few days later was still an awfully sick Masai boy, and being sick saved his life. His throat had been injured badly—a claw had just missed the jugular vein—and he was being fed intravenously, with a nutrient solution that was purely vegetable in origin.

The other Masai in the village, in all the Masai villages, fell ill and began to die. Dr. Chang guessed at least part of the answer even before the arrival of the epidemologists and tried to save them, or some of them, but the disease was new to him and he wasn't a bacteriologist. His advice to them to stop eating food from cattle was good advice but it came too late—and would have been ignored even had it come in time. Most of the victims were too far gone to be eating anyway and the entire tribe, except for one badly damaged boy, was already infected and doomed. The medical reinforcements that arrived found Dr. Chang in a village peopled by the dead and the dying.

But M'bassi lived. After the last other Masai in the village had died and had been buried and after the other doctors had moved on to where they hoped they might still be useful, the Buddhist medical missionary stayed on, alone with the boy, for two weeks longer, until M'bassi could be moved. First to Nairobi for a month in the hospital there, then, convalescent, by rail to Mombassi and by ship back to China.

Back in his native land the good doctor had prospered.

He had raised the boy like a son and had been able to send him abroad for an education. To London, to Tibet, to the Massachusetts Institute of Technology.

§

Meet M'bassi. Six feet five inches tall, and slender. Black as the Venusian night. About forty years old now. Quiet, contemplative eyes set in a fierce African face made fiercer looking by deep scars from the claws of a lion, claw marks that ran from up in his kinky hair the full length of his face, having miraculously missed both eyes. A soft gentle voice that made any language it spoke sound sweet and melodious. Buddhist, mystic, mathematician, and a wonderful guy.

I'd been steered to him by Ellen. She knew him because he had been a friend of Brad's and had suggested him months before, when I'd first mentioned that field theory was one of the subjects I'd need coaching in. Chang M'bassi —he'd taken his foster father's name and, in the Chinese manner, put it ahead of his given name—was an instructor in higher mathematics at University of Southern California.

"But don't," Ellen had told me, "let the 'instructor' part fool you. He can have a full professorship any time he wants one. It's just that he doesn't want the responsibility and doesn't want to put in that much time; he'd rather be an instructor because he can put in less time at it, have more time for his own work."

"In that case," I said, "why would he be interested in coaching me?"

"He might not, Max. For purely monetary considerations I'm sure he wouldn't. But if you got to know him first and the two of you liked one another—"

The two of us liked one another.

God knows why. Except for one thing—and that one thing was something I didn't learn about until I'd known M'bassi a long time—we seemed to have nothing, absolutely nothing, in common. Mysticism bored me to tears. Science, except for the pure realms of higher mathematics, held no interest for him.

But somehow we became friends.

§

In October I took my degree in rocket engineering.

We had dinner and a party, quite a party, in a suite at the Beverly. Rory and Bess Bursteder flew down from Berkeley for it, Bill and Merlene from Seattle. Klockerman and his wife. Chang M'bassi, stag. Ellen of course. Nine of us.

Bill enjoyed himself, but I think he was a little baffled at most of the conversation. Still, he was pleased and happy to be there. Pleased not so much by the degree I was celebrating as by the fact that I'd finally got the dirt and grease off my hands, that I finally was holding down a responsible position and getting somewhere. Klockerman's little speech announcing that arrangements had been made for me to become assistant director at the rocket port got a big hand from Bill. But I caught Merlene looking at me curiously and I winked at her to make her even more curious. It does a woman good to be curious and it served her right for being smart enough to realize that a leopard doesn't change its spots without reason.

§

Christmas eve alone with Ellen, at her place. I'd shot the works on a present for her, a pearl necklace. I'd been, for almost a year now, earning more money than I'd ever earned before. And behaving myself, with little chance to spend much of it. Money piling up in the bank had begun to worry me and this was a wonderful excuse to get rid of a chunk of it.

Ellen gave me a beautiful cigarette case, a black one studded with chip diamonds in a random design. Random? I looked again and it was a familiar pattern. The Big Dipper, Ursa Major, pointing to Polaris, the North Star.

She said, "The only way, darling, I could find to give you the stars."

I wanted to cry. Maybe I did cry a little; my vision blurred.

1999

1999

From Ellen in Washington, late January: *"Oh, my darling, my darling, I wish you were here with me tonight. Or that I were there with you.*

"Then this tiredness and this dull headache would go away. Then I'd be happy and relaxed. But headache or no, I've got to tell you what I accomplished today.

"I picked my victim and my timing perfectly. The victim: the Gentleman from Massachusetts who is the leader of the conservationists and the head of the appropriations committee, Senator Rand. The timing: a tête-à-tête lunch for which I cleverly lured him to a spot where neither of us was known, so there would be no interruptions.

"And while we ate I bored him stiff, telling him the advantages to science and humanity of a close-up look-see at big Jupiter. But that was just the surface subject. Underneath it I kept dropping stronger and stronger hints that I could and would push that bill through despite opposition. I intimated that I already had enough votes lined up to carry it—not true, but he'll never find out now—and that his opposing it wasn't going to do him any good. I watched him get sourer and sourer about it while I kept mentioning how small a figure three hundred and ten million dollars was for such a project. To keep that figure fresh in his mind, I mentioned it half a dozen times.

"I waited till we'd finished lunch and were sipping

brandy; Rand always tops off a meal, even lunch, with a brandy so I did too this time. While he was savoring the warmth and flavor of his first taste of it, I mentioned casually that there was another way of getting a rocket to Jupiter, much more cheaply and with the additional advantage of a landing on one of the moons. I took your prospectus, the one you and Klocky did together, from my purse and showed it to him. He didn't look at anything but the figures, but he really stared at their total, only twenty-six million. And then he stared at me. 'Senator Gallagher,' he said, 'if it can be done this cheaply, why on Earth or Jupiter did you introduce a bill based on a figure twelve times as high?'

"I'd known that would come, of course, and had my answer ready—that the technique for doing it more cheaply had not been worked out at the time I presented the bill now in the hopper and that the step-rocket covered in the original bill had the advantage of being a two-man rocket and provided more space and comfort for the spacemen who would man it. But that in spite of those factors I would be willing to withdraw the original bill and substitute one based on the inexpensive one-man rocket if, but only if, I had his personal word that the conservationists would let the substitute bill go through without delay and without opposition. They wouldn't have to vote for it, I pointed out; they could abstain or take a walk in the corridor while the bill was being voted on.

"He stalled a while, trying to tell me that he could promise nothing more than that he himself would not oppose the bill, but I pooh-poohed that and flattered him a bit by *telling him I knew how much influence he had with the conservationists in both houses and telling him I knew they all looked to him for leadership. He still demurred and I got on my high horse; I told him that if we were going to have a fight on our hands anyway we'd make the fight on the basis of the original and more expensive proposal, and fall back on the alternative only if the original bill lost out. He saw the light, finally. He promised to do his best to see that there was no active conservationist opposition if I withdrew the original bill and introduced the substitute. And Senator Rand, whatever you may think of him otherwise, is a man of his word.*

"The bill is practically passed, Max. It was already drafted and I turned it in this afternoon. It'll be reported out of committee next Monday. We'll get it voted on in the Senate within a few days, get it through the House of Representatives within a month at the outside.

"And it won't be vetoed. We have President Jansen's private assurance of that, and given on the basis of the original bill. He'll sign the substitute one like a shot. And be so pleased to get off so cheaply that I'm sure he'll agree to appoint whomever I suggest, provided he's politically qualified, for project director. And before I suggest anyone for the appointment, Max, I'll have the suggested one's private promise to make you his assistant director.

"So in about a month, say around the first of March, I suggest you have Klocky start that vacation of his and leave you in charge. A three months' leave should be ample time; your appointment should be made and confirmed by then, although the project itself isn't likely to get started,

even on the drafting board, until fall. The boys at White Sands are going to have to vet the plans and that will take time. There is, there had to be, a provision in the bill that makes the feasibility of the rocket subject to their approval before the appropriation is actually made and the project set up for operation.

"But I don't anticipate that they'll cause any trouble. In fact, I'm reasonably sure they'll not only go along but be enthusiastic about giving us all the help they can. General Rudge, the big noise there, was in Washington last week end and, strictly off the record and in confidence, I showed him your prospectus. And he told me, also unofficially, that it looked good to him, although of course they'll have to check the figures forty ways from Sunday and I have a hunch they're going to insist on upping a few of the safety factors a little.

"Well, that's the score to date, darling. Wish it wasn't so long till the midsession recess, seven long weeks. But by then probably the bill will be passed and signed—with luck your appointment will have been made and confirmed. Then we can really celebrate, no?

"Meanwhile, don't forget to Write Your Congressman."
I wrote my congressman that I missed her like hell.

§

And I *was* missing her like hell. Being away from her was showing me that I really loved her and that what was between us was something deep and important, not just an affair, like others I'd had. Sometimes I almost damned Project Jupiter for keeping us apart.

"Alone—and I'd never felt alone before—I found that there were too many evenings in a week.

It was a very rainy rainy season in Los Angeles, but I walked a lot, sometimes having to wade in flooded streets. I read a lot. As often as I could without boring them I spent evenings with Klocky or M'bassi, arguing or playing chess. I heard an occasional concert, took in a few shows. Still there were too many evenings. Seven of them a week.

Why did I love Ellen? It was like asking why I had five fingers on each hand.

The days rushed by, at work, and the evenings crawled.

§

From Ellen, early February: *"My telegram of yesterday told you that the bill passed the Senate, darling. Quite probably, if you were sticking as close to the viddy for news as I suspect, you knew it even before my telegram got there.*

"But I doubt that any of the newscasts carried a breakdown of the vote, so you probably don't know how close a thing it was. It scared us, and it's changed our plans a little.

"Max, it passed by a margin of only three votes.

"And it wasn't because Rand crossed us up. He didn't. Of the approximately twenty-five votes in the Senate that make up the conservationist bloc, only a few went against

us; nearly all of them either were absent at the time of the voting or abstained.

"And we had twenty-five certain votes lined up on our side—the fifteen we can always count on and ten more that we'd traded for. We'd figured that, as usual, the other fifty votes, the in-betweeners, would divide about equally. And if that had happened we'd have had almost a two to one majority with the conservationists abstaining.

"But even with no organized opposition, with no speeches against the project, those in-between votes went heavily against us. The actual vote was 36-33, which means that out of forty-four votes cast besides the twenty-five we were sure of, we got only eleven, one vote out of four.

"Since then we've found out why, by talking to some of the in-betweeners who usually vote our way, who are usually willing to go along with any expansionist project in reason. There'd been a sudden change of sentiment because of that Mars rocket crash last week, the three-million-dollar rocket carrying cargo and six men for the Mars colony that was hit by a meteor and crashed on Deimos.

"I'd heard about it at the time, of course. I'd even known that there was what I'd thought was a mild popular furor over it, but I'd never suspected that men supposedly intelligent enough to be sent to the Senate of the United States would be swayed by that furor. As though we'd curb surface transport because of one train crash, no matter how much money it cost or how many people it killed!

"So although, thank God, the bill did go through, we got a scare that showed us how overconfident we'd been. And we learned that before we let that bill be reported out of committee and voted on in the House, we've got to plan carefully and move cautiously. We've got to go in for horse trading on a big scale.

"And we're going to have to wait, in any case, at least until after the recess and possibly even a month or so longer, until that rocket crash is less fresh in the minds of the representatives and their constituents. If, God forbid, there's another rocket crash within the next couple of months, we'll simply have to keep that bill in committee until we can try to jam it through on the closing day of the session. And it would be pretty much of a gamble even then.

"So if Klocky hasn't made irrevocable arrangements to start his leave on the first of March, it will be better if he waits a month and starts the first of April. Please ask him to, because I've got a selfish reason, too, for wanting it that way. The midsession recess this year will be the second two weeks in March, from the sixth through the twenty-first. If Klocky leaves the first of March you'll be holding down his job and I know you wouldn't be able to take those two weeks off. But if he stays on through March, could you possibly, so soon (although it seems so long) after the week we had in Mexico City?

"I still have this damned headache, although it isn't as bad now as when I wrote you last. Now that the excitement about the appropriation bill is temporarily over, I think I'll go to a doctor about it; hope it isn't migraine, although they've got pretty good techniques for taking care of that now so it'll be nothing to worry about seriously even if that's what it is.

"Do let me know as soon as you can about those weeks, so we'll have time to make plans if you'll be free."

It was all right with Klockerman; he'd made arrangements and plans to start his leave the first of March, but it wasn't too late for him to change them. I telephoned Ellen that evening and we had a long talk. We picked Havana, Cuba; we arranged to meet there on the sixth of March.

The narrow vote in the Senate and the delay necessary before the bill could be brought before the House didn't worry me seriously at all. If anything they made me more optimistic. Things had been going *too* smoothly, *too* easily, I'd felt. A hitch or setback of some sort had been due and overdue. Now that there'd been one and it hadn't been a fatal one, I felt better.

§

Lunch one Sunday with M'bassi, rabbit food for him and a steak for me. Afterwards since it was a sunny afternoon and unseasonably warm for February even in Los Angeles, we went to one of the nudist beaches to sun ourselves for an hour or two. I, to get an early start on the tan I wanted to acquire. M'bassi because he loved the sun and its warmth; God knows he didn't need a tan.

We talked of lions. M'bassi brought them up.

"Yesterday afternoon," he said, "I did a thing that I have never done before. I went to a zoo. I went there to look at a lion. I had not seen a lion for thirty years. I saw one."

"What did it look like?"

"It looked like a lion. It looked very much like a lion. But for a while I suspected that it was not one, because it looked so different, so utterly different, from the lions I had seen as a boy in Africa, so utterly different from the lion that had saved my life by mauling me. Then I realized that the difference was not in the lion but in my perspective on the lion. It was an odd experience. I am glad that I went."

"The difference in perspective," I said, "could be due to either of two things. The difference between a free lion and a caged one, or the difference between the viewpoint of a boy and the viewpoint of a man. Which was it, M'bassi?"

"It was neither of those things, Max. It was the difference between the viewpoint of a savage—for at eleven years I was a savage—and that of a civilized man. It was more than the difference between the viewpoint of a boy and of a man because had I remained a savage, continued tribal life, that viewpoint would not have changed."

"How would you define that viewpoint? That of the savage, I mean."

"Admiration, respect, and the desire to kill. The need to pit my manhood against his lionhood in combat, to prove to myself that I was not afraid of him."

"But I thought the Masai were so brave they were not afraid of lions."

"Of course they were brave. And of course they were afraid or there would have been no bravery in their lion hunts. Where there is no fear there can be no bravery."

"And your attitude toward a lion, as a civilized man?"

"Admiration, respect, and compassion."

107

"It's easy to feel compassion for a caged lion. What if it had been charging you in Africa?"

M'bassi sighed. "I would have defended myself, if possible, with regret. The Hsin philosophy is not fanatical; it recognizes that although all life is important a human life is more important than that of an animal."

"Then it wouldn't be a sin to kill a charging lion. But it would be to hunt one?"

"Under certain circumstances that too might be necessary. If, for example, a lion has become a man-killer. What would be wrong would be to hunt or to kill for pleasure, to take joy in the death of any living creature."

Living creatures, sea gulls, soaring lazily and gracefully overhead. Living creatures, a group of girls, walking by, giggling and jiggling. The lazy rhythm of the waves, the sun's warmth and the sky's blueness.

I waved my arm at it. "All this, M'bassi. All this and the stars too. Isn't it enough without having to invent a religion and a God?"

"It might be, if we could *have* all this and the stars too without a religion. You have science. I have religion. You back your horse to take you to the stars; I'll back mine."

I didn't dream, then, that he meant it.

§

I pretended that I was rich and took the Miami rocket, flew the rest of the way to Havana. Ellen's jet landed two hours later and I was able to have a hotel suite ready for us by the time I met it.

Ellen had seen a doctor about her headaches; he'd fixed them up and everything was fine. But she seemed tired the first few days.

"Damn it, woman," I told her, "you've been working too hard. You've done more than your share on the Jupiter project already. Let the starduster lobby jockey it through the House."

"I'll be pushing it too, Max. I'll be all right, all rested up, by the time I have to go back. And my tiredness isn't *all* from pushing a rocket toward Jupiter. That Buckley Dam bill—I've got to get it through for California or I won't have a ghost of a chance of being re-elected."

"And why do you want to be re-elected? Ellen, it was you who pushed me into administrative work but I'll have to admit I'm through disliking it, and it pays well. Well enough to let me afford a senator of my own. Why don't we get married as soon as my appointment is set?"

"We can talk about it then, darling."

"We can *do* it then," I said. "We can *talk* about it now. There's no charge for talking. Ellen, are you in politics because you really want to be, because you really want a career for yourself? Or just to make a living?"

"I—Max, I honestly don't know. It's probably a little of both and right now I'm too mixed up to analyze my feelings about politics or about getting married. In any case I wouldn't want to marry you until after I've finished the term I was elected to—and that's another two years. It's a long time."

109

"Damn right it is. And we're not getting any younger."

"No, but we're not missing anything either, are we? We're together almost as much as if we were married. Max, even if we married sooner than two years from now I wouldn't resign from the Senate, so I'd still have to be in Washington six or seven months a year."

"At least you wouldn't have to wear that damn mask in public."

"I don't mind it. And think how nice it is to take it off when we're in private. Will you make us drinks?"

She sipped hers and then lay back against the pillow and closed her eyes. "Talk to me, darling."

"About what? About how much I love you?" I frowned at her. "Damn it, woman, do you know this is the first time in fifty-eight years I've ever asked a woman to *marry* me? And I can't even get a straight answer out of her."

"I love *you,* Max. I'm yours. Isn't that enough? Why, you're a part of me. What do a few words and a piece of paper matter?"

"It isn't the words and the paper. It's—oh, hell, I guess it's selfish of me, when you make me analyze myself. It's probably mostly because I want to be able to brag about having you, not have to keep it secret."

"Secret, except for the few people you really care about. Klocky, the Bursteders, your brother and sister-in-law, M'bassi, a few others—"

"All right," I said, and tried to think of another reason, one that would make sense.

Ellen beat me to the punch. She sat up and reached for her drink again. "Max, let me explain you to yourself.

I'll believe that you never asked another woman to marry you, but don't ask me to believe you've never loved another woman. You must have, more than once, and at least as much as you love me. Now admit that much."

"Sure, I've loved other women. But never as *much;* you're wrong there. This is different."

"Max, I'll tell you what's different about it. You're space-nutty and you have been ever since you were old enough to know what love was. By the time you did know, the stars came first and the woman second. Marriage would have tied you down and kept you from trying to go where you wanted to go. Now and for the first time, you've got the two things in one package—a woman you love and through her a chance to help send a rocket farther out into space than one has even gone before."

There was a hell of a lot of truth in that.

She said, "If you doubt that, I can prove it to you. Suppose I offered to marry you right now, here in Havana, but only on the condition that you'd quit looking up at the stars and dreaming about them."

"You wouldn't ask that. You wouldn't be *you* if you did."

"Of course not. But you see my point just the same. Oh, Max, let's not talk about marriage tonight. Let's not *us* talk about anything. Just you talk, and let me listen."

"All right. What shall I talk about?"

"The only thing you talk well about, the stars. Do you really think we'll ever reach them?"

"You're just baiting me, darling. You know perfectly well that I really think we'll reach them—and that we really will. It's only a question of time. Don't ever sell mankind short by saying there's *anything* he can't do, ever, or anything that he isn't going to do.

"The stars are there waiting for him and he's going to take them. Someday, and maybe suddenly, he's going to explode into deep space as he exploded into the solar system in the sixties. Only let's hope this time he doesn't have to wait until he's scared into it."

"Scared into it?"

I said, "Yes, like the Germans and the Japs scared us into developing the A-bomb. Like the Commies scared us into starting the space station and shooting for the moon. Sometimes it looks as though we have to have the bejesus scared out of us before we're willing to tackle anything that has to be tackled on a big scale and that takes a lot of billions of dollars to accomplish.

"The Nazis and the Japs in the forties—before your time. You know why we developed the A-bomb? To save money. The Nazis we could have licked without it—in fact, we did, because it wasn't developed in time. But the Japs were set for a long bitter defense of their homeland and it would have cost us more billions than the A-bomb cost us, to defeat them with lesser weapons. Wait, that's not entirely true—although it worked out that way. When we *started* developing the A-bomb we weren't thinking about saving money; we were thinking about saving our way of life and maybe our lives; we were scared to the point where money didn't matter.

"And it was in the fifties and the early sixties that the Commies gave us an even worse scare—before the rift between Russia and China in sixty-five and the counter-

112

revolutions in the other satellite countries ended our worries about them. But in the late fifties—and I'm old enough to remember them—we were scared spitless of the Commies. They had A-bombs too, so that wasn't enough. That's when we really started pouring money into trying for controlled atomic energy, energy that could be used for power and propulsion as well as for sheer destruction.

"And before we'd even got it we were shooting the moon by starting work on the space station, starting to put it up there in the sky with chemical fuel rockets, Ellen, primitive three-stage affairs that stood as tall as a ten-story building, and whose pay load was only a fraction of a per cent of their take-off weight. It took us three years and four or five billions of dollars to get the *first* ton of pay load up in that orbit. All of that on chemical fuel rockets before the nuclear boys came through and step-rockets were as obsolete as crossbows—and so was the space station, for military purposes, before we had it well started. Why, instead of one space station up there we could have orbited thousands of rockets with H-heads, controlled by radio and ready to blast a whole continent off the earth if we wanted to.

"Only before we put them up there, there wasn't any need to. Communism came apart at the seams and we weren't scared."

"But we went on to the moon and Mars just the same, Max."

"And Venus," I said. "Our momentum carried us that far and no farther. We weren't scared any more, and big spending stopped. An observatory on the moon, a small experimental colony on Mars. A few looks under the clouds of Venus. And there we stopped."

"Maybe just to catch our breath, Max. That was a big and sudden jump."

"Forty years is too long a time just to catch your breath in. We're overdue to push on. Not just to Jupiter and the outer planets, but to the stars. We should be trying for the nearest star anyway."

"But could we, Max? Right now, I mean, with what we've got, with what we know?"

"We could, yes. It would cost plenty—maybe as much as the atom bomb and all our planetary rockets put together. It would have to be a *big* ship, assembled out in an orbit like the space station was. It would have to be big enough to hold at least half a dozen families, to be practical, because by the time that ship made the four light-years to Proxima Centauri at our present speeds, it would be their descendants several generations later who'd get there."

"Yes, I remember now reading about how it could be done. But I'm afraid, darling, people aren't ready for anything like that yet. Spending all that money, all that effort, and then never knowing what the result would be because they'd be a century dead before the results could be known —if they ever were."

"I know," I said. "It could be done, but I know it won't be done. Not for centuries, anyway, if that's the way it has to *be* done. I wouldn't vote for it myself."

Ellen opened her eyes. "*You* wouldn't?"

"No, I'd rather see those billions thrown into developing

an ion drive. Why, if the government put the money and effort into that that it put into developing the A-bomb—why, they might find it in a few years! And you and I might be still alive when the first ship came back from a star!"

Ellen's eyes were bright. "Maybe, if something spectacular comes from the Jupiter trip—"

"What— Wait, something spectacular could come at that, Ellen. Uranium—our resources aren't too high on that, and if we found a lot of it on one of Jupe's moons—that could be one thing. Or intelligent life. I think that would be better than uranium. To *know* there was intelligent life—waiting for us out in the galaxy—Ellen, that would stimulate our curiosity, our drive to get there, more than anything else would."

"Would it? Mightn't it work the other way? Make us afraid we might find life *more* intelligent than ours?"

"I don't think so. Men may be cowards individually, but collectively maybe that's just the challenge we need. God, if we'd only found canals on Mars, proof that another race besides ours *had* lived!

"Just for lack of fuel to feed it on the first few places we reached, are we forgetting our big dream? Are we forgetting where we started to go?

"Jesus, do we have to wait till a matter of survival for us to do it? Until we get scared again? Until a space ship from some other star system comes here and starts shooting us up so we've got to have star ships to fight back? Or until our astronomers tell us that our own sun is going to nova and explode, and give us a deadline date to get away from it? Or—a dozen million years from now—decide our own sun is getting so cold we'd better find another one before we freeze to death? Ellen, do we have to wait for one of those things?"

She didn't answer and I looked over at her. She was breathing slowly and regularly. Sound asleep.

I turned out the lights and got quietly into bed without waking her.

§

The second week she felt much better, much less tired. We went out more that week, saw the town. Neither of us cared for dancing but we both liked good modern Cuban music, the quarter tone stuff that America had imported in the seventies and discarded in the eighties but that was still going strong in Havana. We liked Cuban dancing, too; I guess we were both old-fashioned.

We took a couple of boat trips on the sunniest days, renting skitterbugs, those little skimmers that are so fast you have to wear bathing suits because of the spray. Out of sight of shore we'd stop and let it rock in the waves while we took off our suits and sunbathed on the flat part of the deck. There aren't any nudist beaches in Cuba; people of Spanish descent are for some reason awfully prissy about nudity, like Americans used to be.

It was a good vacation and we both felt fine, all rested up, when it ended, as it had to end. Ellen back to Washington, I back to the L. A. Rocket Port.

And to a plenty busy week. Klocky's last week before his vacation leave, one week to show me the various things I still didn't know about taking over his job while he was gone. We worked late every evening as he'd remember one thing after another that I should learn about.

It's a big job, I was learning, running the Los Angeles Rocket Port, plenty of responsibility and a hell of a lot to know about every department under you. Until Klocky got back I was going to be up to my ears in work.

He left for Africa on the first of April. I saw him off in a gray dawn. "Keep in touch with me, Max, so I'll know when the appointment is set and it's okay for me to come back. But not sooner than three months, damn it. I want at least that much time off. And—good luck."

§

For a while, until I got things licked into shape so I could handle them, I was too busy to worry about my luck. But it was still holding.

I heard from my congressman late in May:

"Hold thumbs, darling. We're going to run the bill through the House late this week, Thursday or Friday. That's definite, unless, of course some rocket disaster, inter-planetary or local, should happen sooner. We'll postpone a showdown if that should happen; we don't want another near thing such as happened in the Senate. We want to be sure; we want at least a sixty per cent majority.

117

"And we've been working hard and we're sure we'll get in and without waiting any longer.

"So that you won't be distracted these last few days, spending all your time watching the viddy for news, count on a telephone call from me the minute we know for sure. My call will be made before you'll get even a flash in the viddy, because it's not a big enough deal—to the commentators—for them to put on a flash until the vote is final, but I'll phone you as soon as we know it's in the bag and not wait for the exact count or the last few votes.

"The bill won't be voted on before ten in the morning nor after five in the afternoon, Washington time, and that's 7 A. M. and 2 P. M. your time, so be within reach of a telephone between those hours on Thursday and Friday if you want the news as quickly as I can get it to you. If the call is before nine (your time) I'll try your apartment first, after that I'll call you at the port.

"It's going to be good news, darling, believe me. And here's another item of good news. I was at the White House yesterday, with two other senators and talking to the President on another matter, but I managed to get a few minutes alone with him after we'd finished what, to everybody else concerned, was the main order of business. I brought up the Jupiter project and reminded him of his assurance to us that he'd sign the bill if Congress passed it. He remembered and reassured me that he would.

"And he said he'd heard about it when it had passed the Senate and had been surprised at the fact that the appropriation figure was only twenty-six million, that he didn't remember the exact figure that had been mentioned when *the bill had first been discussed with him but he had the impression that it had been a lot more than twenty-six million.*

"That gave me a perfect opportunity, Max, to start laying my groundwork for your appointment. I told him something about you and gave you full credit—except that I told him Klockerman had checked your prospectus and figures—for working out the less expensive way of doing the job.

"And while the iron was hot I did a little more ironing with it then and there. I told him that I thought you should be, and deserved to be, director of the project. I admitted, though, that it might be wiser to have a politician for that job, one who knows the ropes and the red tape, as the nominal director, but that whoever got the directorship should get it with the understanding that he should make you his next in command, with the title of project superintendent, and let you handle the actual construction of the rocket.

"He agreed with me, darling! He said that any man who could figure how to cut a three hundred million dollar project down to less than a tenth of that amount certainly deserved to work on that project if he wanted to, and in the highest ranking job he was capable of filling.

"In fact I had to fast-talk him out of deciding then and there to make you director instead of superintendent. And that wouldn't have worked, darling, and here's why: his appointee to the directorship will have to be approved by the Senate and there's too much of a chance for a wheel to come off in that deal. You're not a known political figure and so there'd be sniping at you by some senator or other

who wanted to get the job for someone he owed a political obligation to.

"And the sniping would take the form of questioning your qualifications and you know where that would lead. It would bring out the fact that your engineering degree is less than a year old and that until only a year and a half ago you'd had no experience in administrative work at all. And that would mean to the Senate, and to the President too when the word got back to him, that you're not qualified to direct a multimillion dollar project. It's much too big a risk to take. And your being suggested for the directorship and turned down would make it awfully rough for me in getting you the job of project superintendent, if I could do so at all.

"So I told Jansen I didn't think you'd even want the directorship; I told him you'd be much more interested in the actual engineering and construction, that you cared more about rockets than about paper work. I told him you'd been both a spaceman and a rocket mech and knew rockets from the ground up to as high as Mars and that, anyway, a politically known figure ought to front for the project as director.

"He asked if I had anybody in mind for the top spot and I said I'd thought of several good possibilities but that I'd rather not make a specific suggestion until after passage of the bill by the House, and I told him when that was scheduled.

"He asked if its passage was certain and when I told him that it was, he called in his secretary and his appoint-

*ment calendar and made a date for me to see him at two
o'clock Wednesday, a week from tomorrow.*

*"By that time I'll have picked out the stuffed shirt I'm
going to recommend for director and also have a second-
string one in reserve in case Jansen makes any objection
to the first. And I'll have talked to both of them, with cards
on the table, and will have told each that if I recommend
him for the job it's going to be in exchange for the promise
to name the man I suggest as his project superintendent
and that if he won't promise I won't recommend him for
the directorship.*

*"He'll promise all right; I worked out that bill so that
the directorship is a plump political plum (How's that for
alliteration?) with good pay. And the prospects I have in
mind are going to want it badly enough not to quibble
about the single condition I attach to recommending them
for it.*

*"Things are snowballing to a fast finish, darling. Hold
thumbs."*

§

I held thumbs. Ellen's letter had come by rocket mail
and special delivery; it reached me early afternoon of the
day she'd written it, Tuesday.

So I had two days of thumb-holding to face if the bill
came to a vote on Thursday, three if it held over till Friday.

And I really held thumbs. I was getting scared again,
now that it was so close.

So many things could go wrong.

What if there was another rocket crash? There hadn't been, since the Deimos one which had come so close to wrecking the passage of the bill through the Senate. I'd caught a late roundup newscast every night so I was sure. But what if there'd be one now, in the last few days before the bill was passed? It would stall things till next session for sure and might even change the whole picture. At the best, almost a year's delay. And I wasn't getting any younger; I'd just passed my fifty-ninth birthday. Sixty coming up.

Those last few days I kept a pocket viddy on my desk at work, catching every newscast that came on. Especially Thursday, while I was expecting a call from Ellen. After all, she might have trouble getting a call through and the viddy might beat her to the news. I didn't stir out of my office without first making sure my secretary would know exactly where to reach me if a call came from Washington. But none came.

I waited until I got back to my apartment to phone Ellen; it would be nine in Washington then and she'd be sure to be home. She was.

"Everything okay, darling?" I asked her.

"Everything's fine. Bill's scheduled for tomorrow, third on the agenda. The first two are pretty routine matters so it ought to come up by eleven o'clock; that's eight A. M. your time. You'll still be home then, won't you?"

"Yes, but—but if you call much later than that I'd be on my way between home and the office. So here's what I'll do. I'll go to the office early, get there at seven o'clock, say.

Then whenever you call I won't be enroute between the two places."

Her soft laughter came over the wire. "All right, I'll call the office then. But you needn't get there before half past seven; I'm sure the bill won't be passed any sooner than that. And then only if we can keep it routine and avoid debate."

"Fine. I'll be at the office from seven-thirty till I hear from you. Ellen, your voice sounds tired. Are you all right?"

"I *am* tired. Outside of that, I'm all right."

"No more headaches?"

"No more headaches. And I'll rest up now. I'm going to bed early tonight. Tomorrow I'm not going to the Senate. I'll be in the gallery of the House, watching, until I phone you, and then I'll take the rest of the day off."

"And rest?"

"And rest. Oh, maybe I'll go somewhere in the afternoon, just for relaxation, if the bill goes through in the morning session. Tell you what I'll do. Go to the zoo and watch the monkeys. After a morning of watching the House of Representatives, that will sooth my nerves. And restore my faith in human nature. Or simian nature, if there's any difference. Darling, I wish I had your faith in humanity."

"You have more than I. You're just overtired. And I won't keep you any longer. Good night, darling."

I tried to go to bed early that night, myself, but I was too keyed up, too worried, to get sleepy. After a while I gave up, put on a lounging robe and went up on the roof to use my telescope a while. Jupiter was below the horizon

123

but Saturn was beautiful that night, at just the angle that best shows off the rings. Spectacular Saturn, next out beyond Jupiter, our next step outward after Jupe.

And tomorrow would tell the tale of whether we'd be going to Jupiter soon. Would the bill go through, or would a wheel come off?

§

No wheel came off.

Ellen's call came a few minutes before nine o'clock. "All okay, darling," she said, "it's going through."

"Wonderful."

"A comfortable margin. It's a roll call vote, still going on. Only about three-fourths of the House has been polled but we've got a majority already—a majority of the total number of votes that will be cast, I mean. So it's really passed already. If you're interested in the final count I can phone again in about twenty minutes."

"It doesn't matter," I said. "Ellen, you still sound tired. You'd better go home and rest up. Or were you being serious about going to the zoo this afternoon to watch the monkeys?"

"I was about halfway serious when I said it, but I guess I'll go home and get some sleep instead. I've got a dinner-date tonight. It's time I start lining up my recommendations for the directorship."

"Who, tonight?"

"Whitlow. William J. Whitlow. He's my first choice. Does the name mean anything to you?"

"It sounds familiar but I can't place him. Brief me."

"Ex-congressman from Wisconsin. Jansen's own party. He lost out in the last election but it wasn't his fault; he ran well ahead of his ticket, got more Wisconsin votes than Jansen did. There was that scandal out there, remember, about the dairy interest briberies. Whitlow wasn't involved but too many of his party were and too many straight ticket votes went against him. In the House two years ago he led the fight for the Alaskan reclamation bill—it had his name on it, the Burns-Whitlow Act. That's where you probably heard of him."

"What's he doing now?"

"One of the undersecretaries of state. That was the best job Jansen could hand him after the election, but it's not much of a job compared to the directorship of the project, pays about half as much and gets him only a fraction as much publicity. He'll jump at the Jupiter project. And Jansen will be glad of a chance to move him up; I'm sure of that."

"Nothing against him that might come up when the Senate has to approve him?"

"Not a thing. He's kept his nose clean. Dull and almost disgustingly honest. He won't get a single challenge in the Senate. He's a natural, Max."

"Sounds good. But how about conservationist tendencies?"

"I've checked his voting record carefully. He's better than middle of the road. Hasn't been active in pushing any expansionist bills, but he hasn't voted *against* a single rocket or colony bill. That makes him a lot better for the job—more politically acceptable, I mean—than if he was known as a fanatical expansionist."

"Right. What's he like personally?"

"Well, a bit stuffy, I'm afraid. But don't worry; you'll be able to handle him and he won't interfere with you. He doesn't know the first thing about engineering or rockets, not even about construction. He'll be glad to take the glory and supervise the paper work while you do the real job. I'll do a good job of selling you to him tonight. No, come to think of it, I won't mention your name tonight. I'll just get his irrevocable promise to make the person I name his assistant in exchange for my recommending him for the directorship."

"Why work it that way?"

"I've got a scheme that ought to make it doubly sure. Really Machiavellian. If I hold off on telling him your name until after he's talked with Jansen about the job, just maybe Jansen will remember some of the things I told him about you and suggest you on his own hook to Whitlow. And a recommendation from Prexy would make Whitlow think he's in an embarrassing spot because of his promise to me. And then when I recommend the same man Jansen had recommended, just look what it will do to your stock with Whitlow! He'll be so happy to be able to keep his promise to me and still take Jansen's advice that you'll own the project; he'll be afraid to cross you on anything. And if Jansen doesn't mention your name, nothing's lost."

"Good girl," I said. "Don't let him keep you out late tonight."

"I won't. Won't have to. I'll be offering him a deal he'll jump at, not trying to sell him something. I won't even have to be nice to him, let alone try to seduce him."

"You'd better not. But that reminds me—don't you think this deserves a celebration? Today's Friday; I can fix things to be off tomorrow and Sunday. If you sleep all this afternoon, all night tonight and all day tomorrow do you think you'd be rested up enough for a celebration, just the two of us, tomorrow night? I could take a stratojet there tomorrow afternoon and catch one back Sunday afternoon."

"It sounds wonderful—but Max, let's wait until we can *really* celebrate, until your appointment has been made. If I really push things that could be as soon as next week end, and isn't that worth waiting for?"

I sighed. "I suppose so. But it's damned lonesome here, with Klocky gone too. I see M'bassi once in a while, but I can hardly celebrate with him this week end. He won't drink anything stronger than wine and only a glass or two of that."

Ellen laughed. "Doesn't sound very festive, does it, darling? Why don't you run up to Berkeley tomorrow night and hang one on with Bess and Rory? They're wonderful people."

"They are, and I will," I said.

"Oh, and don't miss tonight's papers, Max. We've got a really good publicity man and he's worked out fine press releases on the project. We've been holding them back

127

until it went through the House, but he'll release them this afternoon."

"I'll watch for them," I said. "All right, darling, I won't keep you talking any longer. I hope I'll see you next week end then, and keep me posted."

"I'll let you know the minute there's any further news. 'Bye now."

§

I intended to phone Rory that evening to make sure he and Bess would be at home and free the following night and that they'd want me to come up. But Rory beat me to the punch. He phoned me at the office just before quitting time.

"Max, can you run up here for tomorrow evening?"

I said that I could.

"We're throwing a wing-ding to celebrate Project Jupiter," he said. "About fifty of us in on it so far, mostly the boys at Treasure, but there'll be more. We're taking a suite, or as many suites as we'll need, at the Pleiades Hotel and it's going to be quite a brawl."

It was quite a brawl all right. It lasted till dawn. I found that I was the guest of honor because the newspaper releases had given me most of the credit for working out the plans for the rocket. I had to make a speech and botched it badly, but nobody seemed to care.

§

The publicity hadn't hurt my stock at the L. A. Rocket Port either. I found that out Monday morning when I went back to work. If there'd been any resentment—and I'd thought there had been at least a little—about the way Klocky had jumped me up so fast, over other people's heads, it was gone now. I was hero for a day now, and I could do no wrong. I could feel the difference.

No word from Ellen Monday or Tuesday. No reason why she should have called or written, of course. A newscast Tuesday afternoon mentioned that the President had signed the Jupiter Project bill and that it was now officially enacted. But that had been anticipated so there was no reason why Ellen should have called me about it.

But Wednesday was the date of Ellen's appointment with Jansen, and I knew she'd phone me, or at least send a telegram, as soon as she left him. If she'd made the deal with Whitlow and if Whitlow was definitely going to get the appointment, then I was in.

Her appointment was at two o'clock, eleven Pacific time, so after eleven I stayed in my office so as not to miss a call. When it hadn't come by noon I sent out to have a lunch brought in to me and stuck by the telephone. By one 'clock I was getting a little worried; surely her appointment with Jansen wouldn't have lasted more than fifteen minutes. Then I decided she must have had to hurry back to the Senate and had decided to call me this evening.

But five o'clock, when I was ready to leave work, was eight o'clock for her and still there'd been no call. Don't be a damned fool, I told myself; no news is good news. Everything went okay and she's waiting till you're home to phone you so the conversation can be leisurely without interrupting your work.

I ate hurriedly enroute and was home by six. At seven I phoned Ellen's apartment in Washington and got no answer. I tried again every hour until it was two o'clock there, eleven to me, and gave up for the evening. If she wasn't home by two she was staying elsewhere for the night. But why hadn't she called me? Surely she'd know that I was waiting for a call and might call her if she didn't call me, and that I'd wonder and worry when I found she wasn't home.

I set the alarm for five and turned in. I got a little sleep off and on, but I got up at four-thirty and made myself coffee. I tried her apartment again at five; if after spending the night out she came home to change clothes or get papers to take to the Senate with her, that was the time she'd be home, an hour before the Senate opened. No answer; she hadn't come home at all.

I made myself wait an hour and a half, then I phoned the Senate, now half an hour in session, and got the sergeant-at-arms. I had to pull my rank as director of the port to convince him my call was important enough for him to go to her desk on the floor of the Senate right away. I told him, though, that if she was there he didn't have to pull her away to answer the phone if she was busy, but that he could give her a message to call me back as soon as convenient, and that I'd hold the phone until he came back and told me whether he'd found her or not. He came back on in ten minutes and said that Senator Gallagher had not yet come in, but that he'd watch for her and give her my message when she did come.

I thanked him and hung up.

Should I try the Washington police? If she'd been in an accident it would have been last night, in all probability, and they'd know by now. But if everything was all right, if there was a simple explanation for her absence, a call to the police might start an inquiry that would prove embarrassing to her, might even make the newspapers or a telecast before she turned up.

I sat staring at my phone. It rang.

Washington was calling. I breathed again, thinking Ellen had just reached the Senate, had had my message from the sergeant-at-arms, and had called right away.

But it was a man's voice. "Mr. Andrews?"

I said yes.

"This is Dr. Grundleman of Kerry Hospital. I am calling on behalf of Senator Ellen Gallagher, who is a patient here and who asked me to make this call."

"What's wrong? Is she badly hurt?"

"It was not an accident, Mr. Andrews. She is to undergo an operation later today for the removal of a brain tumor. She asked me to tell you—"

"Save the message for a minute. How dangerous is the operation?"

131

"It is a serious one but the chances are fairly good. They would have been much better had the operation been performed ten days ago when the condition was first diagnosed. But I think we can bring her through."

"What time's the operation? Can I get there in time to talk to her before it?"

"It's scheduled for half past two; we'll have to start preparing her for it at two and it's nine-fifty here now, our time, so that means there's only four hours and ten minutes. I suppose a chartered rocket would do it, but that would be terribly expen—"

"Tell her I'll be there," I said. I slammed down the receiver.

I picked it up and dialed the home number of my secretary. After a few minutes she answered sleepily.

"This is Max, Dotty," I said. "Snap awake because this is an emergency. Got paper and a pencil handy?"

"Yes, Mr. Andrews."

"Good. Write these things down so you won't slip up on any of them, and start doing them the second I hang up. First, call the port and tell them to get the charter rocket ready to take off the minute I get there; it'll be within twenty minutes. If there's more than one pilot on stand-by, I want Red. Landing clearance at Washington. Got that?"

"Yes, Mr. Andrews."

"Second you've finished that, get a helicab to pick me up here. Emergency priority, pilot to land on the roof. If he gets in trouble for it, I'm responsible. I'll be on the roof in ten minutes after I finish this call. Listen, get those things started happening while I get dressed, then phone me back and I'll give you a few more."

I threw on clothes. Dotty called back just as I finished. The rocket was being readied and the helicab was coming. I gave her instructions about the port itself this time, who'd be in charge and what to tell him, things like that.

Then I ran up three flights to the roof, got there two minutes before the helicab landed to pick me up.

§

We took off from the rocket port at seven-twelve, just twenty-two minutes after I'd hung up on my long distance call from the hospital. The trip to Washington—with maximum acceleration and deceleration allowed on a passenger flight—should have taken two and a quarter hours. But Red didn't figure me for a passenger, when I told him that every minute counted. We let down in an hour and fifty minutes. And there was a hellie waiting for me; it came right out on the field to pick me up the moment we'd landed. I hadn't thought of that, but Dotty had.

So I reached the hospital by noon, Eastern time, two hours before they'd start preparing her for surgery.

At the desk they wouldn't tell me Ellen's room number. Dr. Grundleman had left orders that I was to be shown to his office on arrival. I was shown to his office.

He was red-faced, short and stocky, bald as the nose of a rocket; he looked more like a bartender or a wrestler than like a doctor. He held out a hand and I took it but I didn't hang onto it long. I hadn't come to see him, but to see Ellen, and would he please have me taken to her.

"You made excellent time getting here, Mr. Andrews. There's no hurry."

"You're not in a hurry, but I am. Where is she?"

"Please sit down, Mr. Andrews. You won't lose any time with her by sitting down a moment here. It's almost two hours before we must start preparing her, and I cannot possibly let you have more than an hour with her. Even to let you spend that long is stretching things. And wouldn't you rather have the last hour, from one until two, so you can be with her right up to the time when we'll have to start preparing her?"

"All right," I said. "Providing you let her know right away that I'm here and that I'll be with her at one, so she won't lie there wondering if I'll make it in time or not."

"She already knows. The desk phoned me while you were being brought here and I immediately relayed word of your arrival to Senator Gallagher; she knows that you are here and that you'll spend the hour from one to two with her. Now will you sit down?"

I sat down. I said, "Sorry, Doctor, I'm edgy."

"Which is another reason why I'd rather you didn't see her immediately. I want you to be calm, not excited, when you talk to her. Do you think you can be?"

"I think I can pretend to be," I said. "What happened? When and how was she brought here? How long has this been going on?"

"The tumor must have started developing at least a year ago. The first symptom, headaches, started develop-

134

ing in January. At first they were intermittent and not too severe; Senator Gallagher went to a doctor for treatment late in March, about two months ago."

I nodded. That would have been immediately after our vacation in Havana. She'd probably been more ill then than she'd let me know.

Grundleman was saying, "The doctor she went to diagnosed the trouble as migraine and treated it as such. No fault of his; the location of the tumor is such that the symptoms at that time were almost identical with those of migraine. And for a while she seemed to be recovering. Until ten days ago there was a sudden setback, one that made her doctor suspect his original diagnosis and suggest that she come here immediately for a thorough examination. We discovered and located the tumor and I advised an immediate operation. She insisted, however, on waiting two weeks, despite the increased danger the wait would entail, until she had finished with some legislative business she considered extremely important."

I closed my eyes. Jupiter project. She'd considered it important enough to risk her life for. Or had it been the project itself, rather than my driving interest in the project and her love for me? "Go on," I said.

He shrugged. "There was nothing I could do. We scheduled the operation for this coming Saturday. Arranged to have Dr. Weissach—do you know of him?"

I shook my head.

"Probably the best brain surgeon in the world. Lives in Lisbon, but has no practice of his own, just operates. Where possible people are flown to Lisbon for him to operate on, but in an emergency case like that of Senator Gallagher he will come to the patient, although at a much higher fee."

"Any question of money?"

"Oh, no. Senator Gallagher can meet all expenses. Dr. Weissach is already here. He arrived this morning and has made his preliminary examination and arrangements. He is resting now. Is there anything else I can tell you?"

"Yes. What are her chances?"

"With a surgeon like Weissach, I would say they are excellent."

"How long after the operation before she is out of danger, *completely* out of danger?"

"I would much rather answer that question after the operation."

"All right. I'll have to phone my office to let them know how long I'll be gone, but that can wait."

§

I walked into Ellen's room at one o'clock exactly.

She looked pale, otherwise no different from the way she'd looked when I'd last seen her. She smiled up at me. I didn't kiss her, not yet, not just then; I just stood looking down at her. Striking, her chestnut hair on a white pillow.

She must have realized that it was. "Take a last look at the hair, darling," she said. "They're going to shave it off, you know."

"To hell with your hair," I said. Maybe not a romantic

136

first remark, but she knew what I meant and smiled again.

"Woman," I said, "why didn't you let me know this was happening? You've known for ten days you were going to have an operation."

"I didn't want you to worry. Oh, I wanted you here, wanted to see you once more before the operation—in case. But the operation was to be this coming Saturday; I was going to phone you Friday evening and have you come on a night plane and be with me Saturday morning, and Sunday you could have gone back. This way—I'm sorry it was such short notice, darling. But I'm so glad you came anyway. Aren't you going to kiss me?"

I kissed her very gently, tenderly.

She said, "Now Max, pull up that chair. Sit and let me talk till I've brought you up to date. Dr. Grundleman said you didn't even let him give you my message."

"I didn't want to waste time, that's all. I just wanted to get here. What was the message?"

"That President Jansen will appoint Whitlow, and that Whitlow has made the promise I asked him to make."

"Woman, why didn't you have that operation ten days ago when Grundleman said you should have it? That Jupiter rocket is going to take a couple of years to build anyway, so what difference would a few more weeks make?"

"I couldn't have stalled it then, Max. It was lined up to go through the House, everything set and ready. It would have gone through from there without me."

"But then why didn't—"

"Don't you see, darling? I'd have been out of circulation

at just the wrong time, when the appointments were being made. And I wanted you to have that job. Besides, I thought Grundleman was exaggerating the danger and the need for rushing into an operation. I thought two weeks more wouldn't matter, that it wouldn't involve any additional risk. And if it was going to kill me anyway, I wanted to make sure you'd have what you wanted, what we both wanted you to have."

"Quit talking as though you're going to— Damn it, woman, you're going to be okay."

"Of course I am. But I had to consider the other chance. Here's what happened yesterday. I saw Prexy at two and I took a short cut by bringing Whitlow with me. Of course I left him out in the anteroom when I went in. I got right down to business by telling Prexy who I thought would be the best man for the job and he was pleased. He said he thought Whitlow would be ideal and that he deserved a better spot than the one he had in the State Department. Yes, he'd be glad to appoint Whitlow to the directorship. He'd ask his secretary to make an appointment for Whitlow to see him.

"I grinned at him and told him I'd been so sure he'd like the idea that I'd taken a chance and brought Whitlow with me, that he'd allowed fifteen minutes for my appointment and only two had been used up and why couldn't he save himself another appointment by telling Whitlow now? So he had his secretary bring Whitlow in, and that was that. Except, darling, for the best part! Prexy remembered about you and suggested you to Whitlow for the supervisor job, gave you quite a build-up. While he was doing it—" Ellen giggled a little, "—I could see Whitlow beginning to sweat because he'd promised to appoint whoever I suggested for the job and here was Prexy putting the pressure on him. Then he happened to glance toward me and I nodded. You should have seen the relief on his face, Max. He almost stuttered, he was so eager to tell Jansen that he'd appoint you."

I said, "That's wonderful, Ellen. But why didn't you phone me—I don't mean about that, but when you decided to have the operation today instead of Saturday?"

"I didn't decide. When we left the White House Whitlow offered to drop me home in the cab he was taking and I took him up on it. I passed out in the cab and the next thing I knew was when I woke up here this morning. Whitlow had had the cab rush me to an emergency hospital; at the hospital they found a receipted bill from Dr. Grundleman in my handbag and phoned him right away for instructions. He arranged to have me transferred here and phoned Weissach in Lisbon to come as soon as he could. When I woke up this morning everything was arranged. All I could do was to ask Grundleman to phone you right away, as he did. I hoped you'd come and could get here in time, but in case you couldn't make it I wanted you to know that everything was set about your job on the project."

I said, "Thank God I got that message in time to come."

"I'm glad you did, but we could have talked anyway. After I knew you were coming, after it was too late, I realized that I could have had them run an extension phone in here and that I could have told you myself. If you hadn't been coming, I'd still have had them arrange for the phone call."

"This is better," I said. "I couldn't have kissed you over the phone."

"Nor held my hand. Hold it, Max, because now that you're here there are still a few things I want to tell you."

I moved my chair closer and held her hand in both of mine.

"They can wait till afterward," I said. "For now, just tell me again that you love me."

"You know that already. I've never been as close to anybody as I have been, still am, to you. It's—it's almost as though I'm you and you're me; we're part of one another."

"I know," I said. "I feel it too."

"But if I should—if I don't come through the operation, don't let it throw you, darling. You've got a job to do, whether I'm with you or not."

"Woman, don't talk about—"

"Max, we've got to face the fact that there is a chance I won't come through. Whether it's one chance in ten or one in a hundred, there are a couple of things I want you to know. Will you let me say them, and then we won't talk about the possibility any more."

"All right," I said. "Get them over with. I'll listen." I tightened my grip on her hand.

"First, about my will. I wish I could change it in your favor, but—"

"My God, woman," I said, "I don't want to hear about your will."

"You said you'd listen. I want you to understand why I

140

didn't change it, despite the fact that it's in favor of two distant relatives with whom I'm only on casually friendly terms, although they're the closest relatives I have, even though they're both relatives by marriage, Ralph Gallagher's brother and sister.

"The main reason is the fact that if, when my will is probated, the news gets out that I left you my money, such as it is, it would prejudice your chances of getting that job. If some columnist picked it up and made something of it—"

"Okay, I understand."

"And besides it's not going to be enough to get excited about after paying for this operation, and after funeral expenses and—"

"My God, woman!"

"We're discussing *ifs*, darling, and if I die there's going to have to be a funeral. And that's the other thing I want to tell you about. I don't want you to go to it."

"Why not? There'd be hundreds of people. Nobody would couple our names just because—"

"That's not why, Max. It's just that I wouldn't want you to. I hate funerals, think they're pompous and silly and disgusting. I hate the thought of having one myself even though I won't know about it while it's happening. Since I'm a public figure I suppose there'll have to be one, but I don't want the only person I really love there sharing in it. If I die, I don't want you to see me dead, either here or in a funeral parlor. I don't want you to remember a dead body or even the outside of a coffin. I want your last memory of me to be as I am now, alive. I don't want you even to

141

think about a funeral or send flowers. Will you promise me those things, Max?"

"Yes, if you'll quit talking about them."

"All right, I'm through being macabre. From now on we'll be bright and cheerful. How much time have we got left?"

I glanced at my watch. "Nearly half an hour."

"Good. Now you do the talking for a while. Tell me a story."

"A story? I'm no good at telling stories."

"A true story. There's one you promised to tell me once and never have. Do you remember?"

I shook my head.

"Last October when you got your degree and we had a party to celebrate and your brother Bill and his wife came down from Seattle, remember? Bill made a crack about sewing machines and you laughed with him, and when I asked you what the joke was you said it was a long story, about something crazy you'd done once, and that you'd tell me sometime but not just then. I never remembered to ask you about it afterwards until this morning I thought of it for some reason after I knew you were coming and decided to ask you if we had time."

I laughed. "It's not much of a story, Ellen. I just didn't want to take out time to tell you in the middle of a party. It started with a book I read in my teens, one of the early science fiction novels. I forget who wrote it but it was called *Mad Universe* or something like that. One of those alternate time-track stories, where the hero gets switched somehow to another universe that's been identical with his up to a certain point in history and at that point there's a split in the time-track; something happens in one universe that doesn't happen in the other and they go in different directions.

"In this one the change had started early in the nineteenth century with the accidental discovery of a method of interstellar travel by a scientist who was trying to rig a little low-voltage generator out of an old treadle sewing machine. Had a couple of small coils mounted, the treadle to turn one inside the other, and started it going—and the sewing machine disappeared. He'd had it hooked up wrong—wrong for a generator, that is—but he was able to figure out where he'd made his mistake and tried it again, on his wife's good sewing machine. He lost that too.

"But he kept on experimenting and losing sewing machines until he had the secret of the instantaneous space-warp drive. Ever happen to read the book, Ellen?"

She shook her head slowly.

"You might get a kick out of it, while you're getting better, if I can find a copy, but I doubt if I can. It's probably been out of print for forty or fifty years and I'm not even sure of the exact title. Only way I could get hold of it would be through a collector of early science fiction.

"But anyway, I read it in my teens and didn't think about it again until I was in my early forties, when I happened to get hold of an old copy and read it again. And one thing about it looked different to me then, because I was different and things were different.

"I was a pretty bitter guy about that time, Ellen. I was bitter about the fact that I was only a one-footed rocket

143

mech and would never get into space again and that I wasn't getting anywhere, but I was still more bitter about the fact that *we* weren't getting anywhere. We'd got to the moon and Mars and Venus, and because we hadn't found plains strewn with gold and diamonds or alien aborigines or civilizations, we'd almost lost interest. We weren't going any farther, it looked like, in my lifetime, and in particular we weren't shooting for the stars, weren't even trying to work out a stellar drive. The conservationists were worse then, Ellen, than they are now. We're gradually, I can see now, getting our second wind and getting ready to try again. But that was about the worst point of reaction against space travel and the government seemed on the verge of even pulling in the outposts we already had. Even terrestrial rocketry was at its lowest ebb. A big passenger rocket had just crashed into a crowded Paris street and had killed over a hundred people besides all its own passengers, and there was even talk of banning rockets completely for terrestrial travel. That was in—I think it was in nineteen eighty-four."

I frowned at the way I was telling it. I said, "Damn it, I'm trying to tell you something funny, something crazy I did, and I'm going at it all wrong. But now that I've messed it up anyway I might as well finish filling in the rest of the background. I was drinking a lot then, regularly and heavily. Well on my way to becoming a lush. Rory was trying to straighten me out, and so was Bill—Bill was still single then and living in San Francisco—but I was pretty blue and discouraged and neither of them was having much luck working on me.

"And then one night, getting drunk alone in my room, I happened to reread that ancient book with the thing about the sewing machines in it. And I got to thinking, why not? We didn't, and still don't for that matter, know the basic principle of any form of interstellar drive except the rocket, but there must be one. And since we don't know how it will work we're quite as likely as not to come across it accidentally, aren't we? Only we might speed up the time of that accidental discovery by deliberately messing around with screwy coils and hook-ups.

"I had half a bottle of whisky left when I decided that. I poured it down the drain and went to bed. And the next morning I went to the bank and drew out every cent I had, about a thousand bucks. I quit my job by telephone and I moved to another room in a different part of town so neither Rory nor Bill could find me.

"Then I went out and bought—God help me, Ellen, but this is the truth—three used sewing machines. One of them an electric portable and two old-fashioned treadle ones I had to find in antique shops and pay fancy prices for. And a flock of electric and electronic stuff, wire, coils, condensers, vacuum tubes, transisters, switches, crystals, batteries, everything I could think of.

"I holed in that room and tried random crazy circuits and contraptions fifteen or sixteen hours a day for two weeks. I went out only to eat, and I didn't take a single drink." I grinned. "Maybe that was what was wrong. Maybe I'd have been more lucky—or more intuitive—if I'd combined that spree with a drinking spree, but I didn't. You'd think I'd have found *something*, if not an interstellar drive, out of the tens of thousands of crazy things I tried, but I didn't. At the end of the two weeks all I'd accomplished was to go broke and burn myself a few times with a soldering iron.

"And that was when Bill finally found me and walked in on me. I started explaining to him what I'd been doing or trying to do, and I started laughing because suddenly I was seeing the whole thing in perspective—or maybe seeing it through Bill's eyes—and I realized how howlingly funny it was, so I howled, and after a while Bill got the joke and was howling with me.

"Anyway, it cured me of the long black depression I'd been in, and somehow it brought Bill and me closer than we'd ever been before. That evening, after I'd fixed things to start back to work the next day and had borrowed money from Bill to live on until I got a pay check again, Bill got a little drunk with me, something he doesn't often do. But it was a happy drunk I had, and a mild one, not the escape drinking I'd been doing up to two weeks before. I was out of that."

I grinned at Ellen. "Well, that's the story of the sewing machines. It's been a joke between Bill and me ever since, and he seldom misses a chance to kid me about it. Now you can kid me too."

Ellen smiled. "I love that story, darling, but not because it's funny—although I suppose it is. I love it because it's *you*, and I love you so I love it. Only you're wrong about one thing."

"What's that?"

"We *have* got an interstellar drive. It's in you, and people like you. It's even in me a little, now that I've caught it from you. It's in Klocky, in Rory, in almost everybody that works with rockets. Even in M'bassi."

"M'bassi?" I must have looked blank. "He's no star-duster. He's a mystic."

She smiled again. "Maybe you've never asked him what he's mystical about. Try it next time you see him."

There was a light tap on the door and Grundleman came in. "Just another minute," he said. "Thought I'd give you that much warning." He stepped out and closed the door again.

"Max, darling, promise me something?"

"Anything," I said.

"If I die—we know I won't, but if I do—promise me that you won't let it throw you, won't let it start you drinking."

"I promise."

The door opened again, this time not Grundleman but a nurse and an orderly. The orderly said, "I'm sorry but you'll have to leave now, sir. We're to prepare the patient."

To prepare her, to shave her hair, her lovely chestnut hair so beautiful against the white pillow. I bent down and kissed her hair, and then her lips.

§

Dr. Grundleman came to me in the waiting room.

"They're taking her into Operating now, Mr. Andrews," he said. "Dr. Weissach is ready. But she may be on the table a long time, and you won't be able to see her for at

147

least twenty-four hours after the operation, if that soon. You'll be more comfortable at a hotel, and I can phone you as soon as—"

"I'll wait," I said.

I waited.

I wished that I could pray. Then I did pray, *God, I don't believe that you exist, and I believe that if you do exist you're an impersonal entity and that if you notice the fall of sparrows you don't do anything about it, on request or otherwise, but if I'm wrong, I'm sorry. And in case I'm wrong I pray to you that . . .*"

§

Years later, Grundleman came back. He was smiling. Thank God, he was smiling.

He said, "A beautiful operation. Weissach worked a miracle. I think she'll live."

I stared at him. "You think she'll live! A beautiful operation but you only think she'll live."

He quit smiling. "Yes, she has an even chance now, or slightly better than even. But she won't be completely out of danger for three or four more days."

Jesus God, I thought, what had the odds been before? What had the odds against her been while I was talking to her only two and a half hours ago? What does a doctor mean when he says a patient's chances are excellent? That it's one chance in a hundred or one in a thousand?

"Will I be able to see her tomorrow?"

148

"Perhaps. It's too soon for me to promise that for sure. Phone me tomorrow morning."

"I'll phone you as soon as I check in somewhere, so you'll know where to reach me."

He nodded.

§

In my room at the hotel I discovered how tired I was. I hadn't slept much the night before and the strain of worry is more tiring than physical labor.

But before I let go, I phoned the rocket port and talked to the man I'd put in charge there, told him I'd probably be away a week, and made sure everything was going smoothly and that he'd know where to reach me if he needed help or advice.

I called the hospital to let them know where I was, and then I slept. But fitfully; every slight sound from outside wakened me because my ear was tuned to the telephone, listening for it to ring, hoping it wouldn't.

It didn't.

But even fitful sleep adds up over a long enough period, and morning found me rested and feeling better. And hungry as hell because, I realized now, I'd completely forgotten to eat the day before.

I called the hospital and was told Ellen had had a quiet night and that her condition was good. Grundleman hadn't come in yet so I couldn't ask about visiting Ellen. I left word to have him call me as soon as he came in.

I phoned room service and had a triple-sized breakfast sent up to my room so I wouldn't have to get away from the telephone. I ate all of it.

Grundleman phoned a little after nine o'clock. He told me that Ellen was "resting nicely."

"Is that double-talk or does it mean that the odds are better?"

"Much better. They're definitely, strongly in her favor now."

"Will I be able to see her this afternoon?"

"Probably. Want to phone me about one o'clock? Or are you going to stay in your room where I can reach you?"

"Both," I said. "I'll be here if you want to reach me, and I'll phone you at one if I haven't heard from you sooner."

I knew he wouldn't be calling back right away so it was a good time for me to try to reach Klockerman in Africa, which might tie up my phone for a while. I knew he'd want to know about Ellen and I thought too that I'd better let him know that I was playing hooky from the job he'd given me. He might even want to rocket back and take over himself it he didn't think the man I'd put in charge there could handle things.

I knew he was in Johannesburg and told the operator she could probably find out where he was staying by checking with the American embassy there. She could and did; within twenty minutes I was telling him what had happened.

"Thank God," he said, when I'd brought him up to date on Ellen. "It's odds-on now, then?"

"Definitely. But what about the job? I left Gresham in charge. Can he handle it?"

"Hell yes; don't worry about it. I'm not going to. Just keep me posted on Ellen. Call me again if there's any change or let me know when she's out of danger. How's everything on the Jupiter deal? I know it went through okay—we got that news even over here. But I mean your tie-in with it. All okay?"

I told him it was and explained how Ellen had endangered herself by holding off on the operation until she had everything wrapped up for me.

He said, "She's a wonderful woman, Max."

As though he was telling me something I didn't know.

§

Grundleman beat me to the punch. I'd been watching the time to call him at one o'clock and my phone rang three minutes sooner.

He said, "She's doing fine and she's awake now. You can have half an hour with her whenever you get here. But please stop in my office first; I want to talk to you."

"You're talking to me now. Tell me whatever it is now and save me worrying on the way over. Is anything wrong?"

"Not exactly. Physically, she's doing fine, considering the operation was what it was and was less than twenty-four hours ago. But something's wrong with her morale. For some reason she's feeling depressed and pessimistic,

151

much more so than she was before the operation—and God knows there was cause for it then. That's why I'm allowing you as much as half an hour with her. I want you to cheer her up, tell her I told you that the operation was a complete success and that she's past all danger. I told her that myself, but she doesn't quite believe me."

"I'll tell her. But *is* she out of danger?"

"Almost."

"I don't know what *almost* means. Quote me odds."

"Well—as of this moment I'd say she has three chances out of four."

"Right," I said. "That's language I can understand. And I'll do my best to cheer her up. Only I've got a suggestion I want you to consider."

"What is it?"

"That you let me tell her the truth. If I try to lie to her, as you did, she'll know it even more surely than she knew you were lying. Let me level with her and tell her she now has three chances out of four. She'll not only like that but she'll believe it, and it'll do her more good than all the lies I could tell her."

"Hmmm. Maybe you've got something there, Mr. Andrews. Only let's stretch it a little. Say nine chances out of ten."

"The truth or nothing. She'll know if I stretch it."

"All right then, the truth. But remember, don't get excited about anything while you're with her, and don't let her get excited either. If you want to kiss her, do so lightly, and don't let her move her head. But she knows about that."

§

Thick white bandages this time instead of chestnut hair. But she smiled up at me. "Hope I haven't worried you too much, darling."

"You've been worrying me plenty, but don't worry *about* me. How are you feeling? Any pain?"

"No pain, but I feel awfully weak. You'd better do most of the talking."

I pulled up a chair close. "Fine. What shall I talk about?"

"First, have they told you the truth about my chances as of now?"

"Yes," I said, and told her in detail about my conversation with Grundleman on the phone.

Her eyes brightened a little. "Fine, Max. Yes, you were right. It's a lot better to know the real odds, when they're three to one in my favor, than to be handed a line and have to wonder. Three chances out of four; that's better than I'd guessed. I feel better to know the truth."

"I knew you would. All right, anything special you want me to talk about?"

"About yourself, darling. What you told me yesterday, the sewing machine episode, made me realize how little I knew about you except while you were a spaceman or learning to be one. Before you were seventeen and after you became a rocket mech. What was your childhood like?"

"Nothing very exciting. I was born in Chicago, as I told

153

you, in nineteen-forty. In a four room third-story flat over a paint store on State Street ten blocks south of the Loop; that was a tough district then.

"I was second of three children; had a sister two years older than I; she died about twenty years ago. And one brother five years younger—Bill. Our old man was a street-car conductor, and a pretty heavy drinker.

"I grew up as a tough kid, ran with a gang that committed petty crimes and a few that weren't so damn petty. A lot of my childhood playmates ended up behind bars, and I don't mean as bartenders. I guess only one thing saved me from going the same way.

"From the time I could read, I read all the science fiction I could lay my hot little hands on. Comic books—remember them? Then magazines and novels. There was wonderful stuff being written then—or it seemed wonderful to me. Adventures on Mars and the other planets and across the galaxy and to the farthest galaxies. They knew space travel was coming, the boys who wrote those early science fiction yarns. They had the Dream, and they gave me the Dream. There was stardust in what they wrote, and it got in my eyes. I knew space travel was coming and I knew I was going to be a spaceman.

"That's what kept me in line, kept me from going too far astray. I knew I had to keep my name off the police blotter, keep out of the reformatory, or they wouldn't let me in the space corps when one was formed. That's what kept me in school when my friends stayed out, because I was able to figure even then that I'd have to have an education to go where I wanted to go.

"God, the fights I had because I wouldn't duck school with the kids I ran with and they thought I was sissy, or when they thought I was yellow because I wouldn't risk getting a record by helping them roll drunks or burgle stores. Did me good, though; toughened me up and taught me that nothing is easy and you have to fight for what you want. I wanted space, and I fought for it.

"And all the while we were growing up and living under the shadow of the A-bomb, under the threat of all-out atomic war any minute—and I was glad of it, reveled in it. I loved it because I could see even then that it was fear and fear only that would ever make a government spend the billions it would have to spend to get us the space station and the moon and the planets. I didn't care how big a risk we were taking, didn't care how afraid we got to be, if being afraid got us started toward the stars.

"It did get us started, and it's going to get us there. It's in the cards, Ellen. It's something we've got to do, unless we want to become extinct like the dinosaurs. And we won't, because we're smarter than dinosaurs. We're past the stage already where changing conditions can lick us, as it licked them, because we can change conditions ourselves. We can do more to nature right now than nature can do to us. And we ourselves won't retrogress because we've already got a science of genetics—and give us a few more centuries to educate people up to having it applied and the race will never slide backward either physically or mentally. We'll keep it getting stronger and stronger and smarter and smarter until we're gods. Or as near to being gods as we'll ever want to be; we'll have to keep a little of the devil in us to keep us from boring ourselves and one another.

"Ellen, we'll reach the stars all right. If we have to, it'll be by slower-than-light ships that take generations for a crossing, or that send colonists in suspended animation for centuries enroute. But I don't think we'll have to. Relativity tells us we can't exceed the speed of light, but relativity is just a theory, and there's a short cut somewhere. Hyper-space, sub-space, whatever you want to guess it'll be. But if it's there, that short cut, we'll find it. Don't sell us short."

Ellen was smiling at me. "I wouldn't even sell *you* short, Max. And—it's nice to be able to believe with you. I didn't really, at first, but I do now." There was an almost child-like note of wonder in her voice. "We really *are* going there."

"Damn right we are. It's just a matter of time, like our taking the next step out in the solar system, to Jupiter, was just a matter of time. A damn short time now, thanks to you."

"Thanks to both of us, darling. That's *our* rocket. I only wish I could ride it with you."

"Ride it with—?" I stared at her.

She smiled again. "Don't you think I know you by now, Max? Don't you think I know every bit of you and the way your mind works? Don't you think I know you'd give your other leg and both of your arms—not to mention your life —to pilot that rocket yourself, and that you've got enough confidence in yourself to know you could do it? And don't you think I know that you're going to try?"

156

I didn't answer.

She said, "It's all right, Max. I *want* you to, if you can get away with it. Even if you're going to kill yourself doing it, I want you to have that chance, to die that way."

I squeezed her hand. There wasn't anything I could think of to say, anything at all.

"Max, if I die—"

"Damn it, woman, you're not going to. Don't talk about it."

"All right, after this I won't. But—there's an envelope on the stand there. Put it in your pocket."

I picked it up. "What is it?"

"A little of my hair I asked them to save. I didn't want to tell them what a sentimental fool I was, so I told them I wanted a sample so that in case my new hair grew in gray I could have it dyed to match what it had been. But I wanted it for you, Max. I want you to take it with you if you get to make that trip. I want part of me to go too, and I want you to leave it on—wherever you land, whichever moon of Jupiter. You don't think that's silly of me, do you, Max?"

I shook my head because I didn't quite trust my voice.

She said, "You see, darling, if I die, I want you to think of me when you're out there in space, rounding Jupiter. I want to be with you, as nearly as I can."

I said, "Ellen, you're going to live. Get that through your head. But whether you do or not, if I get away with that rocket you'll be with me on the trip every minute, every second, whether I'm awake or asleep. You'll be with me, Ellen, you'll be with me."

§

I still wanted to stay by the phone until Ellen was completely out of danger. So I had dinner sent up to my room again that evening, and some magazines to kill time until I felt ready to sleep again.

The evening passed slowly.

I went to bed and to sleep around midnight and the phone wakened me at three-fifteen in the morning.

Ellen, the phone told me, had just died.

§

I was sitting at a bar. There was a drink in my hands; they were shaking so badly I had to use both of them to hold it. I hadn't tasted the drink yet. I'd just picked it up.

I stared down into it.

I shouldn't taste it, I told myself. If, as I felt now, I took even a sip, I was gone. I'd take a second sip and a second drink, and.

Not this way out, this time. Not the little death of temporary oblivion, the familiar escape. Not this time.

I owed too much.

Ellen had given me too much. Her love. Her life. Our rocket. The rocket would be built now. It would go to Jupiter. But she had wanted me to build it, and she had wanted me to ride it if I could.

158

I couldn't let her down by starting to drink now at a time when starting to drink would mean keeping on drinking and would cost me everything that she had wanted me to have.

And besides, I suddenly remembered, I had promised. I had specifically promised Ellen that if she died I would not let her death do to me what, a moment ago, it had been about to do.

I put the glass back on the bar, and I walked out. I went back to my hotel, back to my room. It was midmorning, ten o'clock. I think I had walked all those hours since three-fifteen, until I had found myself about to drink and the finding had unnumbed my mind.

From my room I phoned Klockerman. I told him.

"My God, Max," he said. "What can I say?"

"Nothing," I said. "Don't try to. I just wanted you to know."

"I'll catch the next rocket back."

"Don't, Klocky," I said. "If it's the funeral you have in mind, she wouldn't want you there because she made me promise not to come to it. And if it's the port you mean, please don't. Let me get back to it and run it a while, for as long as you want to stay away."

"Are you sure that's what you want to do, Max?"

"It's what I've got to do. It's the only thing I can do, Klocky. I'm catching the next scheduled rocket back. I want to get back to work, to work like hell."

§

I never did find out whether Ellen's funeral was held in Washington or back in Los Angeles. I dived right into my job and worked myself crazy, read no newspapers, took sleeping pills every night to knock myself out until I could start working again the next day.

It was almost a month before I began to think clearly about anything except work, the work I'd been using as an anodyne, as a less harmful anodyne than alcohol.

The ache was still there; it would always be there. But I could think now despite it or around it. I began to want to see people again. M'bassi, Rory, Bill had all phoned me but I'd put them off. Klocky had been phoning weekly, ostensibly to check with me on how things went at the port, but actually just to talk to me, to see how I was doing and when I'd be ready to have him come back. The fourth time he called, about the middle of July, I told him, "Okay, Klocky. No hurry on my end, but come back any time you're ready." He said that was swell, that he'd take another two weeks and be back by the first of August.

M'bassi was out of town when I phoned him. The woman he roomed with said he'd gone to Tibet and would be back in another week or two. Rory was home when I phoned Berkeley that evening and sounded happy when I asked him if I might run up to see him and Bess over the coming week end.

Meanwhile, I decided, I'd better brief myself on what,

if anything, had been happening on Project Jupiter. I stopped downtown on my way home from work that evening and picked up back copies of *The Times* and *The Herald* for the past month and took them home with me. After dinner I went through them.

The appointment of William J. Whitlow to the project directorship by the President had been announced three weeks before; confirmation of the appointment, without opposition, by the Senate only a week ago.

That was the extent of the news, but there'd been two Sunday supplement stories about the project, one with diagrams and drawings of the rocket that weren't too far off the track, the other quoting various astronomers and astrophysicists about what conditions would be found on the various Jupiter moons and which would be the best one for the ammonia pick-up landing. Also some wild guesses of the writer's about what form intelligent life would take on Jupiter's moons if any of them held intelligent life. The usual crap.

I decided to phone Whitlow and ask him how soon things were going to get started, and then I reconsidered and decided to wait until Klocky was back; after that I could tell him I was ready to take off on an hour's notice any time he was ready for me.

§

Klocky got back two days early, rested up and ready to

go. As soon as I was his assistant again, and expendable, I phoned Whitlow.

"William J. Whitlow speaking." A dry, pedantic voice.

"Max Andrews here," I said. "Just wondering when we're going to get started on Project Jupiter, when I should give notice here that I'm quitting."

There was a slight pause, not long enough to make me worry. Then he said, "There's no hurry, Mr. Andrews. The first steps are purely administrative and are being taken here in Washington. You aren't needed for them since your job will be the supervising of construction in the field. That will not start till next year."

"Why not?"

"Why *not?* Mr. Andrews, you do not seem to realize the complexities of organizing a project of this magnitude. The financial arrangements alone . . ." His voice trailed off as though he had decided explanation was hopeless.

"What financial arrangements?" I wanted to know. "Congress appropriated twenty-seven million dollars. The President signed the bill and made you director. Is the Treasury too broke to turn the money over to the project?"

"You are being facetious, Mr. Andrews. You know perfectly well that a government project takes time to get into operation."

"Yes, I do know. And I've always wondered why."

I could hear him sigh, over two thousand miles away.

He said, "My dear man, these things involve complicated procedures, very complicated procedures. Forms must be printed—"

"And tape must be dyed red, I suppose. But seriously, can't we get construction started before next year?"

"I am afraid not. In fact, if we get actual construction, past the drafting board stage, started *early* next year, we'll be doing very well indeed. Don't forget that approval of our plans must be obtained on three levels before we can even go to the drafting board."

I groaned. "All right, if it's early next year then it's early next year, but let's move it up if we can. In any case, let's not let it be any later than that. The job itself will take a full year."

"Longer than that, I am afraid."

"It can't take longer than that without overrunning our appropriation," I said. "The cost estimate was based on the job being done within a year. Listen, Mr. Whitlow, there are a lot of details I want to talk to you about—too many to discuss over the phone. How's about my coming to Washington some week end soon? When can you spare me an afternoon of your time?"

"Well—not this coming week end, or the next. The one after that?"

"If that's the soonest. All right, let's make it definite. To save me phoning you again. Time and place?"

"I don't ordinarily go to my office on Saturday, but I suppose I could."

I supposed he could, too; if I was coming all the way from Los Angeles to see him he could travel as far as his office to see me.

I said, "Your office, then. Or—wait, if I catch the early stratojet I'll get in just about noon. Why don't we meet somewhere for lunch, and then go on to your office after we've eaten."

"I already have a luncheon engagement for that day, Mr. Andrews. Can you be at my office at two?"

I told him I could be at his office at two.

Well, Ellen had warned me that he was a little stuffy, hadn't she? Not that I gave a damn about his stuffiness. What was getting me down was the terrific speed with which the Jupiter rocket was not taking off.

Well, I'd argue with him some more about that when I saw him. At least he hadn't shown any signs of forgetting his promise to make me his project supervisor.

§

Still the ache, still the empty feeling as though part of me, the most important part of me, was gone. But now, with Klocky back and the pressure of work off me at the port, it began to drive me to seek company instead of solitude. Some evenings with Klocky, sometimes playing chess, sometimes talking. We worked out a rough sketch and rough plans for a rocket that would make the round trip to Saturn, next from the sun after Jupiter. The mysterious ringed planet; we still didn't know much about those rings and wouldn't until we could observe them at close range. But Saturn, like Jupiter, has moons with ammonia on them, and the same general plan as that for the Jupiter trip could be used. Saturn's a lot farther than Jupiter but we were surprised and pleased to find that a Saturn rocket would cost only about three times as much as the Jupiter one—still peanuts compared to the three hundred million dollar estimate Bradly had made on the plans for the original Jupiter rocket, the step-rocket one. But Saturn would have to wait until the Jupiter rocket had made the round trip and proved itself a success.

The next week end, the one before my date with Whit-low, I flew to Seattle to spend a day with Merlene and Bill. It was good to see them again. Now, with Ellen dead, I'd probably never have a home of my own, and Bill's house would be as near to one as I'd ever know. God, I thought, if I only had a couple of kids like Easter and Billy, Jr. But it had been too late for that even when I'd met Ellen.

Or had it? Ellen, at forty-five, probably couldn't have had children, but if she'd lived and if she had felt about it as I did, we might have adopted one, maybe one about Billy's age. We weren't too old for that; Ellen at least would have lived to see him grow up.

I thought of trying to talk Bill and Merlene into moving to Los Angeles so I could see more of them and the kids, but I remembered that I'd be there myself only a few months longer, until I could get started on Project Jupiter. After that I'd be at the project site, wherever that would be. I wondered if it had been chosen yet and I made a mental note to ask Whitlow about it. If none had been arranged for, I'd be able to make some suggestions.

After dinner that evening Merlene took Easter upstairs first and I kidnaped Billy and took him out on the front porch in the early dark, with the stars just coming out. We sat on the steps and looked at them.

"Uncle Max."

"Yes, Billy."

"Have you got to a star yet?"

"No, kid. Nobody's got to a star yet. But we will. You want to get there, don't you?"

"Gee, sure. Like Rock Blake on the viddy. He gets to lots of them and has fights and everything. Only Daddy says that's fick-shun, it doesn't really happen."

"He means that it hasn't happened yet, Billy."

"And he says it's a punk, junky program for me to watch, but he lets me watch it. Do you think it's a punk, junky program?"

"I don't know, Billy. I've never watched it. But whether it's punky-junky or not, if watching it makes *you* want to go out to the stars like Rocky Blake does, then it's a good program for you to watch."

"Gee, I think so too, Uncle Max. And the Captain Space program too. Gee, this afternoon he was fighting with green people with heads like lions on a plan-net of Sir—Sir—"

"Sirius?"

"That's it, Sirius. Do you think there are really green people like that up there?"

I grinned at him. "I'll show you where you can go to find out, Billy."

And I pointed out Sirius to him, the brightest star in the sky.

§

M'bassi got back the following Wednesday evening. I went to the field to meet his stratojet. I grinned at the way he towered over the other passengers walking up the ramp from the landing area. "Hi, Licorice Stick," I said.

He smiled and his big white teeth flashed. "Max. It is good to see you." Then his face sobered. "I heard the news, about Ellen. I cannot say how sorry I am."

We had a drink at the airport bar. Wine for M'bassi; he drinks only wine and in moderation. Then I suggested my apartment for a game of chess, and we went there.

We took off our coats, and through the almost transparent nylon shirt M'bassi wore I could see that he'd lost weight; his ribs stood out like the ridges of a washboard.

He guessed what I was thinking and smiled. "It is nothing, Max. A ten-day fast, but I ended it four days ago. I am beginning to regain. You've lost a little weight yourself, my friend."

I had, from hardly eating the first few weeks after Ellen's death. But I was beginning to regain now, too.

I got the chessboard and men and while M'bassi set them up I poured us each a small glass of sauterne to sip at while we played.

Pawn to the king's fourth, he moved. I reached for my king's pawn and then remembered.

"M'bassi," I said, "when I talked to Ellen in the hospital she said that even you had an interstellar drive, and that some time I should ask you what you were mystical about. What did she mean?"

"She spoke truly, Max. Our goals are the same. We travel different roads in trying to reach them."

"You mean you're a *starduster?* Why didn't you ever tell me?"

"You never asked me." He smiled gently. "And you would not understand my road because you call it mysticism and call me a mystic, and those words form a curtain through which you cannot see. To call the study of the spirit and its capabilities mysticism is to say that the body of a man is something which we are capable of understanding whereas the mind of man must ever be a mystery to us. And that is not true, my friend."

"But what's that got to do with getting to the stars?"

"Your plan for reaching the stars is to send your body there, causing your body to carry your spirit—I'll call it your mind, so you will not object to the terminology, my materialistic friend—along with it. Mine is to send my mind there, causing it to carry my body along."

I opened my mouth and shut it again.

M'bassi said, "The idea should not be new to you. You have read early science fiction, I know. Certainly you must have read Edgar Rice Burroughs, who wrote the stories of John Carter on Mars—*Princess of Mars*, I believe, was the first, and there were at least half a dozen sequels to it."

"I read them," I said. "They were Godawful tripe."

"If they were Godawful tripe why did you read them?"

"Because I read them before I was old enough to know how bad they were. While I was a kid. M'bassi, you're not trying to tell me you think those stories were *good* ones, are you?"

"No, I am not. Your estimate of their literary quality is, I will admit, entirely correct. But do you recall that there was one thing about them that distinguished them from all of the other early space stories?"

"Not offhand, M'Bassi. What was it?"

"The method by which Burroughs' protagonist John Carter reached Mars. Do you remember that?"

I had to think hard—it had been damn near fifty years ago, back around nineteen fifty, that I'd read Burroughs.

I said, "I remember. He just looked up at Mars one night and wished he was there, and suddenly he was. Of all the—"

"I started to laugh and made myself stop because I didn't want to hurt M'bassi's feeling's.

"Laugh if you wish," M'bassi said. "It does sound funny if you put it that way. And certainly Burrough's method was an oversimplification, but what if it was an over-simplification of something that will someday be possible for us to do? Let me translate into language that will not offend your materialism by calling it *teleportation,* the ability to transport a physical body through space without physical means."

"But there's been no authenticated case of teleportation, M'bassi."

"Nor has there been an authenticated case of travel by means of sub-space or a space-warp or any of the other shortcut methods science fiction writers have predicated to enable themselves to write about interstellar travel. But there is a considerable body of evidence in support of telekinesis, the ability of the mind to affect physical objects without physical means—to control dice, for example. Teleportation is merely an extension of telekinesis, Max. If one is possible then the other is."

"Maybe," I said. "I'll take rockets. I know rockets work."

"Rockets work. For planetary travel, they work. But for the stars, Max?"

"When we get the ion drive—"

"With any drive a rocket cannot even closely approach the speed of light. Unified field theory proves that, Max, no matter how mystical you think unified field theory is. And what of the stars that are hundreds of thousands of light-years away? Are we going to take hundreds of thousands of years to reach them?"

He took a sip of his wine and put the glass back down. He said, "Thought is instantaneous, my friend. If we can learn to travel with the power of thought we then travel with the speed of thought, not like snails at the speed of light or less. If we solve the secret of teleportation, we can travel to the farthest galaxy in exactly the same length of time it would take us to travel a single inch."

The chess game stood forgotten, one pawn moved, for the rest of the evening while we talked. M'bassi told me about his trip to Tibet. It had been to see a famous *guru* there who was studying teleportation. He had studied and fasted with the *guru*.

"And did he teleport for you?" I asked.

"I—would rather not answer that question, Max. Something happened, or else I imagined that something happened, on the ninth day of our fast together. But hallucinations are common after extended fasting. The thing that happened, if it really happened, my *guru* was unable

170

to repeat, so we have no proof and of what I am not certain myself that I really saw, I would rather not talk. You will forgive me?"

I damn well had to forgive him, because I couldn't talk him into changing his mind. The only other facts about it that I could get out of him were that on the tenth day of fasting the *guru* had become so weak that further abstinence became too dangerous for him and the experiment had ended.

"And he is a very old man, Max, one hundred and seven years old. It may be impossible for him ever to try again, in that manner. But if he does I shall have word from him and I shall go to him again immediately, even if I must spend all my life's saving on a chartered rocket to enable me to reach him in time."

I stared at him. "M'bassi, damn your beautiful jet hide, how could you possibly have not told me these things before I asked you? Look at all the time we've spent together and wasted playing chess or talking about unimportant things. Why didn't you tell me?"

"At first, Max, there was a reason. Ellen suggested it when she arranged for me to coach you in field theory. She said that if I let myself be drawn into arguments about interstellar travel, I'd get no coaching done. Since then— well, we had fallen into the habit of discussing other things and it did not occur to me to change things. And I knew that I could never bring you to my way of thinking any more than you can ever bring me to yours. Not that I disapprove of your way. I may be wrong, and your way of reaching the stars may be the only one we shall ever know."

He sighed. "I wish only that I had your faith. It is you, my friend, who of the two of us is a mystic."

§

And then Washington, D. C., two o'clock on Saturday afternoon, Whitlow's office. William J. Whitlow looked exactly as his voice had sounded over the phone. He was small, dapper, precise, stuffy. Middle aged, but old; he'd been born old, you could tell that by looking at him.

"When," I asked him first, "shall I give notice that I'm leaving the rocket port?"

"The first of the year would be a convenient time, Mr. Andrews," he said. He tented his fingers over the immaculate blotter on the desk in front of him and looked at me over them. "I could get you on the pay roll sooner, perhaps, but there is little if anything you can do until we're ready to start construction. And putting you on the pay roll sooner would not benefit you financially. As the project is set up your job will pay no more than you are undoubtedly earning as Mr. Klockerman's assistant meanwhile."

"I don't care about that," I said. "All I want is to get going on that damn rocket."

"We are setting up things as rapidly as we possibly can, I assure you. And once you start, there will be plenty of work for you to do. Perhaps—ah—this idea would appeal to you. I could put you on the pay roll as of, say, the first of November, and you could end your employment with the rocket port as of that date. But since there would be little or nothing you could do during those extra two months it would give you a chance to rest up, to take a vacation, as it were, on pay, before you would start—"

"I don't want a rest or a vacation," I cut in. "And I'm not in the slightest interested in getting on the pay roll before I can start building the rocket. Have you chosen a site yet?"

"No. I've been intending to ask your advice on it. Do you have any specific recommendation?"

"Not a specific one, but I'd suggest either New Mexico or Arizona. And the site should be within easy commuting distance of a fairly large city—Albuquerque, Phoenix, Tucson, El Paso—a city large enough to absorb all the workers on the project and provide living quarters for them without special construction. If we build out in the middle of nowhere, or even near a small town, we'll have to spend money building living quarters for a couple of hundred people, and that would take a big bite out of our budget. One that wasn't figured in."

He nodded. "That sounds sensible. Of the cities you mentioned, Albuquerque has one advantage over the others. It has the biggest stratojet port, with several scheduled flights a day to and from Washington. And I'll have to be going back and forth frequently, so that would be a considerable advantage."

"Good," I said. "Then we should give Albuquerque first choice. Besides, the government owns a lot of land around there and we might find something we can use without buying—not that it'll cost much if we have to buy. There's plenty of land around there too poor even to grow sagebrush; you can buy it for almost nothing. The one thing

173

we'll want to watch out for is to find a good tract that's near a main highway, so we won't have to waste a lot of money on road building. Want me to look over some places on my way back? I'll have all day tomorrow and I might find something. If I do we can go ahead and sew it up and quit worrying about a site."

"If you would care to, certainly, Mr. Andrews. But—I'm afraid we haven't a setup yet to reimburse you for whatever expenses you incur."

"Don't worry about that. It's on my way back and stopping over won't cost enough extra to bother about. Okay, I'll do that and let you know if I find anything. And I'll give notice at the port that I'm leaving as of the end of the year. Anything else we ought to talk about now?"

There wasn't. All the talking we'd done could have been over the phone and much more cheaply. But I'd wanted to see Whitlow and size him up in person.

I wasn't impressed with him, but I was pleased. He wasn't the type of guy who'd get in my hair much once the thing was under way. I had a hunch he'd be spending most of his time in Washington, especially when he found out how damned hot it can get out on those badlands.

I flew to Albuquerque and got there by dusk. I checked in at a hotel that had hellie service and a landing field on the roof, and arranged to rent a hellie for the next day.

§

It was nearly noon when I found it. I knew at sight that

it was perfect. I was flying south along the main highway, 85, about twenty-five miles south of Albuquerque, about five miles north of Belen.

It was to the left of the highway, not far back. An area flat as a lunar *mare*, about a quarter of a mile square, surrounded on all sides by low hills that would give it shelter from sand-laden winds.

A side road, two lane, already led back to it from the main highway and at the end of the road, the near side of the flat area, was a group of half a dozen buildings of assorted sizes. They looked deserted but not dilapidated. It would be almost too good to be true if that site was obtainable and the buildings already on it usable, even if they needed repairs and alterations.

I flew low and once around the perimeter. It was *fenced*, fenced with a high metal barrier just like a rocket launching area. But it hadn't been that; there weren't launching platforms.

The buildings looked like construction sheds, warehouses, one like a power station. I landed near the buildings and walked over. They weren't in as good shape as they'd looked to be from the air, but they weren't bad either; it would cost only a fraction as much to make them usable as it would cost to build new ones.

But what had this site been?

Suddenly it came back to me; I remembered. The G-station!

Remember? If you're old enough to remember the seventies you remember the plans for the G-station and the wide publicity it got.

A super-luxury space station to be put in the seven hundred mile orbit by a cartel of the biggest of the gambling syndicates, a super-duper gambling club for millionaires who wouldn't mind a thousand dollar ferry charge to get up to it for an evening's recreation.

The gamblers had already thrown a few million bucks into the project, in acquiring this site and putting up these buildings for constructing the ferry rockets that would put the space station up in its orbit piece by piece and which would later be converted into passenger ferries to bring up the customers.

They'd just started the first rocket when the crackdown came, when the Harris-Fenlow bill broke the gambling syndicates, and broke a lot of the gamblers too. The project folded before a single rocket had been finished.

But God what a break for Project Jupiter! Why hadn't I thought of this? Why hadn't *someone* thought of it?

Here was at least a two million dollar saving for us in money, not to mention the saving in time in having our site leveled and fenced, our buildings already built and needing only repair.

And either the federal government or the State of New Mexico must own it, on tax foreclosure. It was a thousand to one that no one had kept up taxes on it for over twenty years.

What a break for Project Jupiter.

I spent a couple of hours walking around, looking around. The buildings were all boarded up tightly and nailed shut but I could get a good enough idea of them from the outside, and I got more and more excited at the idea.

I flew back to Albuquerque and parked my hellie on the roof without turning it in, went down to my room and started phoning. A helpful long distance operator got me Governor Romero at his home just north of Santa Fe at Tesuque. He said yes, the state owned the old G-station site. And yes, he'd give me a little time to talk to him about it if I flew up right away. Yes, there was a field adjacent to his home where a hellie could land; he gave me instructions how to find it.

Half an hour later I was talking to him in person; an hour and a half later I was back at the hotel and had Whitlow on the phone to tell him about it.

"Governor Romero thinks it's a wonderful idea," I told him. "It'll take an act of the legislature so he can't make a definite promise, but he says he feels sure we can lease it for free, or for a purely nominal rental, for as long as we need it. Jupiter Project'll bring quite a few millions into the state that gets it and I hinted that if we didn't get the G-station site we'd probably take a site we were considering in Arizona, near Phoenix."

"A good point, Mr. Andrews. A very good point. And you might also have reminded him of the fact that the property, when we turn it back to him after the project is finished, will be considerably more valuable than it is now because of the repairs, renovations and additional construction we'll put on it."

"I did," I said. "Although the only new construction we'll need is the launching platform, and maybe a crane or two. They didn't get as far as cranes or launching platforms. But there's at least as much building and office space as we'll need."

"It sounds very attractive, Mr. Andrews. I'll look into it. Some time within the next month I'll fly out there and make a personal inspection. If it even approximates what you say it is, I'll get in touch with Governor Romero and make the formal application for a lease."

"Why not strike while the iron is hot? Write him airmail tomorrow and make the request formal, so he can go to work on the legislature while he's enthusiastic himself. Nominal rental means a dollar a year. If we get the lease before you make a personal inspection and then you decide I gave you a bum steer, I'll pay the dollar. So what have you got to lose?"

"Perhaps you have a point there, since it may be at least a month before I can find time for a personal inspection. However, I prefer to wait to write to the governor until I have a full report and description of the property from you, in writing. Will you send me such a report after your return to Los Angeles?"

I told him I would, but I did better.

There were still several hours of daylight left. First, I had the manager of the hotel recommend a good private detective and had the switchboard operator get him for me. I told him I wanted a legal description of that property and wanted it right away—I knew Whitlow well enough by now to know that he wouldn't make a move until he had a *legal* description of the property—and that I didn't care how he got it. I told him that this was his bailiwick and not mine and that if he didn't know where such things were kept he could find out. And that if he didn't know whose palm to grease to get access to such records on a Sunday afternoon he could find that out too. All I wanted was that legal description, right away.

Then I rented a big fancy job of an Instaprint camera and hellied out to the G-station site again and took pictures, lots of them. Half a dozen from the air, at different heights and angles. Close and distant shots of the various buildings, the fence, the road, from the ground.

It was just getting dark when I got back. The detective was waiting for me. He'd done better than copying off the bare legal description; he'd worked as fast as I had. He had photostats of the tax liens and the foreclosure papers. A plat map with the property marked off on it; it included, I was pleased to learn, quite a bit of extra surrounding land besides the fenced in area, including almost a mile of frontage on the highway. And best of all he had construction plans of the buildings, showing interior layout. My photographs hadn't been really necessary, except insofar as they showed present condition.

A good man, that detective. I not only paid him off; I took him to dinner with me. I'd skipped lunch in the excitement and I was plenty hungry by then.

After dinner I got myself a public stenographer and dictated a full report, including details of my conversation with Governor Romero, to go with the documents and photographs.

I checked Washington-bound stratojets while she typed, and when she'd finished and we'd made the works into an impressive sized package, I got it to the jet port in time to make the stratojet that took off at nine-forty. I put special delivery stamps on it, sent it to Whitlow's home address.

I grinned to myself, wondering what Whitlow would think when that completely documented report woke him up in the middle of the night, only hours after he suggested that I send it, presumably at my leisure, after my return to Los Angeles. Well, he'd have no excuse now for not writing to Romero the first thing in the morning.

I'd missed the last jet for Los Angeles, but that didn't matter. The first one in the morning would get me there in time if I went right to my job instead of going home first.

Before I went back to the hotel and to bed, I had myself a drink; I thought I'd earned it.

Project Jupiter was looking up. Unless Whitlow muffed the ball, and I didn't see how he could or why he would, Project Jupiter had a site, and to me, a site was a start.

§

M'bassi lived in the Hollywood slums, in one of those hideous dozen-story apartment buildings on Sunset. Dark, gloomy hallways and an old rattling elevator instead of a tube. The whole third floor, about sixteen rooms, had once been a single palatial apartment, now rented and sublet by a strange woman whose grandmother had been a movie star and who lived in the glory of the past, when Hollywood had been a fabulous place instead of a tenderloin.

180

But once you were inside the four connected rooms at the back which M'bassi rented from her, you forgot about the district you were in.

The big main room was completely oriental, beautifully furnished and ornamented with things he'd brought back from his various trips to China. It was a room as exotic as his study was utilitarian—a medium sized room lined on all sides from floor to ceiling with shelves of books and, besides them, containing only a chair and a desk. Another room combined the functions of bedroom and kitchen. The fourth room was tiny and contained absolutely no furniture at all, not even carpeting. It was the monastic cell in which M'bassi did his meditating and thinking.

Over the soft background music—Scriabin this evening —that M'bassi loved to have going while we talked, M'bassi was answering my questions, or trying to.

"*How* does one teleport himself? Max, Max, if I knew that, do you think I would be here?"

"But damn it, M'bassi, you're trying to learn how to do it; you must know how you go about *trying*."

"A thousand ways. All difficult to explain to someone who has not studied the field. Could you explain, to someone who knew absolutely nothing of physical science, how a rocket works?"

"Certainly I could, in a general way. Atomic energy turns liquid into a gas under high pressure which shoots out of the back of the rocket and pushes it."

"Now explain to me how a space warp drive works."

"You know, damn it, we haven't got a space warp drive yet. But we'll get one."

"And you know equally well that I cannot yet teleport myself. So how can I tell you how it is done?"

"What makes you think it can *be* done?"

"There are two reasons why I think it can be done, Max. One is that it is only a logical extension of the already proved and accepted telekinetic powers of the mind. The other reason is that I believe teleportation has happened. Three people whom I know and trust, under whom I have studied have experienced it in one form or another. They have succeeded in teleporting themselves, but only—how shall I say it?—without fully knowing how they did it, without being able to repeat the act at will, without finding the key. No matter how closely they tried to reproduce the exact mental and physical conditions that existed at the time of their successful teleports, they were unable to repeat."

"Are they *sure* they did it the first time?"

"Is one ever sure of anything, my friend? There is always the possibility that one is hallucinating or otherwise mistaken. Are you sure that I am here, talking to you now?"

"But you believe they really teleported?"

"I do. For instance, the *guru* with whom I spent time, under whom I studied, this summer in Tibet, tells me he is certain that he has teleported twice. He is an honest man."

"Let's grant that. Tell me why you think he isn't a mistaken one."

"Because he is a wise man, wise enough to have taken precautions against self-delusion. He told me the precautions he had taken and I believe them sufficient."

"Do you take precautions when you experiment, M'bassi?"

"Of course. Otherwise how would I know that I succeed, if I do succeed? If I am experimenting in the room you call my monk's cell, I lock the door on the inside; that lock can be worked only from the inside. Suppose I succeed— find myself elsewhere. In this room for example. I return and see if that door is still locked from the inside. If it is, then I could not possibly have let myself out, somnambulistically, walked into this room and awakened here."

"You'd have to break the door down to get back in the cell."

"It would be worth it, would it not?"

I said, "I guess it would. But listen, what's fasting got to do with teleportation?"

"The body, Max, affects the mind in various ways. Food or the lack of it, overweariness, stimulants and depressants, all these things and many others affect our ability to think and our manner of thinking. For many centuries wise men—and some stupid men as well—have known that fasting can bring clarity of thought, sometimes vision."

"And sometimes visions, otherwise hallucinations. So can alcohol. I've seen—well, never mind things I've seen a time or two. But I'm sure they weren't there."

"True. Yet, Max, at just a certain stage of intoxication have you never had the feeling that you were just on the *verge* of understanding something of vast importance, of— You know what I mean."

"Damn right I know what you mean," I said. "But it's always the verge; you never cross the verge."

"Is it not possible that under special conditions one might? Although I believe there is more hope in drugs than in alcohol. I intend to experiment with drugs soon."

"You've already experimented with alcohol?"

"Yes. And with smoking opium. I believe I came closer with opium."

"That's dangerous experimenting, M'bassi."

"Rockets are safe?" He smiled as I involuntarily looked down at my prosthetic leg. He said, "Max, I know you'd take *any* chance to get somewhere you want to go. Why shouldn't I?"

That night I went home with an armful of books from M'bassi's library, ones he said were elementary ones.

They weren't elementary to me. They were gibberish as far as I was concerned. At three o'clock in the morning I gave up and went to sleep. M'bassi could try his methods; I'd have to stick to mine. I was too old a dog to learn such new tricks.

Besides, although I hoped M'bassi had something and I respected him for trying, I couldn't quite believe it.

Project Jupiter, Project Saturn, Project Pluto, Project Proxima Centauri—that was for me. The one-fold path, not the eight-fold path.

§

In October Project Jupiter was in the news again. It had leased the old G-station rocket construction and launching site from the State of New Mexico.

It was in the news just briefly on the Wednesday when it was announced but the Sunday papers and roundup-casts gave it a big play, reviving in some detail the story of the G-station's fall from space before it had risen there. There were photographs with some of the stories and I recognized two of them as ones I'd taken from the hellie. I got a credit line on them, "Foto: Max Andrews," but no mention in the story. On the other hand Whitlow was mentioned only incidentally as director of the project; he hadn't given me credit for the idea of using the G-station, but he hadn't claimed it for himself either. That was all right for publicity. The main thing was that Whitlow hadn't muffed the ball.

Project Jupiter had a home.

It wouldn't be long now, and once the project got started I'd be working on it about twenty-four hours a day and that would be good for me, very good for me.

Not that things were too bad now, except for my impatience. I was coming to accept my loss of Ellen and in that acceptance finding that, in a sense, it brought her back to me. Because I could now think about her and remember her with less pain, she was more constantly with me than before, while bitterness and pain had clouded my thoughts and warped my thinking. Now, sometimes, I even talked to her; imaginary conversations, not aloud. I could go to her now, in my mind, for help and comfort when I needed them. And at times I could even think of her as though we were merely temporarily apart, as when she'd been in Washington and I in Los Angeles; think of her as though she was still alive and waiting for me somewhere. And in a sense she was; she lived in my memory and would live there as long as I myself lived.

Even her death, I was learning, could not take her away from me completely. And with that knowledge came peace.

§

November, getting near December. I began to get impatient to get going on that project. I thought, surely by now things in Washington are shaping up to the point where there are discussions going on, plans being made, that I ought to be in on. So I wouldn't be on the pay roll until the first of the year, but to hell with that if I could be helping get things started.

I asked Klocky if I'd be leaving him in a jam if I left sooner than the notice I'd given.

He laughed at me. "What the hell makes you think you're indispensable? I've known you were leaving the first of the year anyway; I've been getting Bannerman ready to take over your job. Damn it, Max, you've been disappointing me the last month or so, up to now. I thought you'd be heading there even sooner. What's been holding you down?"

"Damned if I know," I said. "Maybe the thought that I'd get there and find nothing to do. That'd be worse than sitting it out here."

"If there's nothing you can do, come back. How's about doing it this way? I'll give you a leave of absence—let's see, today's Wednesday—for the rest of this week. Fly to

Washington and beard Whitlow in his den, find out if there's anything you can start doing. If there is, call me up and quit. If there isn't, come back and start in again next Monday, work another month, or however long it's going to be."

"Klocky, you're a swell guy."

He snorted. "You're just finding that out? What are you going to do about your apartment, though? And your books and your tapes and stuff?"

I hadn't thought of it. I groaned a little, suddenly realizing how much junk I'd accumulated in the last two years. "Damn if I know," I said, "about the books and stuff. There's no problem about the apartment; I've already given notice for the end of the year and paid up till then."

"Give me a key, Max. I'll take care of it, have the stuff sent to you at Washington. Or Albuquerque, if you want to wait for it until you're working at the site."

I breathed a sigh of relief. "Swell," I said. "Listen, I won't want it in Washington; I know that. And if I'm not going to be in Albuquerque until after the rent runs out, just send a moving company around to crate the stuff and hold it in storage."

"How's about the telescope? It still up on the roof?"

I nodded. "I'll bring it down this evening. And I'd better either leave a note or tag stuff, so the movers'll know which stuff is mine. Otherwise they might miss something, like those Bonestell originals."

"Don't worry about that, Max. I know which stuff is yours and I'll supervise the crating. Good idea, though, to bring the telescope down off the roof. Why not do it this afternoon, though? You can catch the late afternoon jet for Washington, be there this evening ready for a good start tomorrow morning."

"You mean you don't mind if I take off right now?"

"Hell, no." He looked at his watch. It's twenty of twelve. Start your leave as of noon, twenty minutes from now. Just time for you to have a stirrup cup with me."

He flicked the switch of the intercom that put him through to his secretary. "Dotty," he said into it, "don't let anybody in here for twenty minutes. We're going to be doing something strictly against the rules. Don't even put through a phone call for that long. If anybody calls, tell him I'm out."

He flicked the switch again, and then took a bottle and glasses out of the bottom drawer of his desk. He poured us drinks and handed me mine.

"To Jupiter, Max."

We drank. Then he looked at me and for God's sake there was mist in his eyes. His voice was quiet. "Do you think you'll make it, Max?"

I hadn't told him. He'd guessed, as Ellen had. He knew me too.

I said, "I think there's a chance, Klocky."

"Jesus but I envy you that chance, Max. No matter how slim it is. I'd give everything I've got—"

He refilled our glasses.

§

I packed two suitcases, enough stuff to last me for a couple of months if I had to be in Washington that long before I could get going on the site.

I dismounted the telescope, brought it down and disassembled it ready for crating.

Bad, I thought, looking around me, that I'd accumulated so much. A man should never own more stuff than he can carry in his hands at a dead run. It was bad, but it had happened.

Stratojet to Washington. Helicab to a hotel, and by then it was evening. I considered calling Whitlow at his home, but decided against it.

Tomorrow, in his lair.

I turned in early and got a good long night's sleep.

§

Thursday, nine. Whitlow, William J. Whitlow, my master Whitlow, behind that big mahogany desk, looking at me across it. Then staring down to doodle with a ball-point pen on a block of foolscap.

Saying, "I'm sorry you came, Mr. Andrews."

Not ready for me yet, damn him. I said, "I don't give a damn about the pay. There must be *something* I can start doing."

"It isn't that. I wrote you a letter yesterday. I'm sorry, for your sake, that you came before you received it."

For Christ's sake, for my sake. Did the bastard mean—? Would I hit him, beat him to a pulp with my fists, or get my suddenly aching hands around that fat neck and strangle him, which?

"Your appointment was to have been announced soon. Naturally though, Mr. Andrews, we made a routine investigation of your qualifications. And when the report came in— Naturally, in view of my promise to Senator Gallagher, and of President Jansen's own recommendation of you, I consulted him and he fully agrees with me that—"

I knew, I remembered, I realized, and I died again, and Whitlow wasn't there any more, no face to beat, no neck to strangle, just a Voice, a gray voice out of grayness.

And the Voice was saying it. The Voice was saying ". . . do not know whether you are a psychopathic liar or whether you thought you could get away with a fraudulent claim, but in either case . . ."

The Voice was saying, " . . . true that you graduated from space school as you claimed, in nineteen sixty-three, but the accident that cost you a leg was on Earth, shortly after you graduated, and not on Venus. And because of it you never left Earth, not even as far as the moon, not even as far as a space station."

The Voice said, "I cannot understand, Mr. Andrews, in view of your other qualifications, why you made such ridiculous claims in the face of fact, because they would have been unnecessary. Your degree in rocket engineering, your responsible position at the Los Angeles Rocket Port, despite how recent both of them are, would have fully qualified you for the job, which after all is the construction of a rocket and not the piloting of one.

"But the President agrees with me fully— and so, I am

190

certain, would Senator Gallagher had she known the facts
—that your making claims to have been in space when you
have not is indicative either of basic dishonesty or of psychopathic tendencies, and in either case . . ."

The Voice said, the Voice said.

§

There was a bar and there were other bars, and then I
was in a hotel room with a bottle part full and another
bottle empty, and the room was gray as Whitlow's office
had been gray, and Ellen was there with me although I
could not see her through the grayness.

"Darling," I was telling her, "darling, it's true, I know
it's true, what the Voice said and is saying, but I want
you to understand that I didn't *mean* to decieve you, I
didn't *mean* to lie to you. And that I knew that I was lying
and yet I didn't know, because I'd been lying to others
and to myself so long that—that—"

"You don't have to explain, Max. I understand."

"But Ellen, *I* don't understand. Am I mad, or was I
mad? How can a man come to believe something that he
knows is a lie? And at the same time not believe it, know
that it is a lie, but that it is a lie he has told others and himself for so long that he has forgotten, that he has accepted—"

I said, "Ellen, I must have been mad, insane, after that
accident that kept me out of space just when I was on the
threshold of it. It was an hour, darling, *only an hour*, be-

fore what would have been my first trip into *space*. A month out of school and my first trip came up, and it happened just like I told it to you except that the rocket was getting ready to take off to Venus instead of from Venus back to Earth.

"To Venus, I was going to Venus. Not just to the moon like most first trips, but to another planet, to Venus. And then the accident—and it wasn't the pain or the physical shock; it was the shock of learning that I was Earth-bound, that I'd never leave Earth, never be a real spaceman.

"And the years, the long years, and the fantasy building up in my mind, my mind not able to take the knowledge that I'd come so close to space and missed by a single hour, a single accident that wasn't my fault.

"I was space-nutty, darling. It was too much to take. I still don't know whether I became a psychopath or a fraud. I don't know, maybe something of both. But I didn't mean to lie to *you*. To myself, to others, it didn't matter. But I should never have lied to you."

"I understand, Max. I would have understood then."

"But since I did lie to you, thank God you didn't find out that I was lying. Don't tell me that you could have loved me still had you learned that I was a fraud. Thank God you never learned."

Her hand on my face. Or a curtain blowing?

"Max, I would have loved you still. I would have believed in you still. It wasn't your fault, Max, that you didn't leave Earth. You tried. And kept trying, all your life."

"Not always, darling. At times—always at times like this when I've known, when I've remembered—I've drunk, like

192

I'm drinking now. For bitter weeks, even months, when I've been sane, when the curse of clarity is upon me and I know myself for what I am. Dozens of times, darling, like this time. I was pulling out of one of them, staying in Seattle with Bill and Merlene, when I first heard of you, when I heard you were going to send a rocket farther out, and I came to help you send it."

"And we've sent it, Max. Don't ever forget, that's our rocket, and it's going out, it's going whether you help build it or whether you ride it. A rocket farther out, Max, a rocket to Jupiter, and it would not be going there—not for another decade anyway—if it had not been for *you*. Isn't that enough for one man, one lifetime?"

"No," I said. "The rocket's going, but I'm not."

"Max, put your arms around me, find comfort in me."

I sought her in the grayness and she wasn't there, she was dead and she wasn't there, she wouldn't be there ever again and I could never find comfort in her again. Ellen, beloved, you are dead and your voice is in my mind and only in my mind.

§

Other rooms, a room with hideous big purple flowers in the wallpaper. And in it I had the dream that always led into the nightmare, the dream and the nightmare that I hadn't had for years now. The nightmare the same, as always; the dream that led to it varied a little each time.

This time, of course, Ellen was in it. We were both

193

young, about the same age, and it was back in the early sixties; I'd graduated from space school and I was a space-man ready for my first trip out; we were to be married after my return from that first trip.

I was kissing Ellen good-by and then she wasn't there any more and I was helping ready the big beast—we called rockets beasts in those days—and with a rag in my pocket I was climbing the outside rings because from inside I had noticed that the forward observation port had a dead gnat stuck on it. Our rise through the atmosphere would prob-ably get it off but there'd be a smear left, and I didn't want to have to look at a smear all the way to Venus. I was going to wipe it off and polish that port.

And then the sudden roaring sound and agonizing pain, and without transition the nightmare. I was in a white room, a hospital room. A doctor had the covers folded back from the foot of the bed, doing something down there, changing a dressing.

I raised my head and looked down.

And went into the frozen moment that lasted an eternity, as it always did.

I woke up trembling, soaking wet with sweat.

I got out of there, out of that room with the purple flow-ers in the wallpaper. Because there'd be no more sleep for me that night, little sleep for nights to come. Once the nightmare had started, it would be there waiting for me, just past the edge of unconsciousness. That frozen instant that lasted till the end of time, waiting for me. Only com-plete and utter exhaustion could carry me safely past it.

§

Streets and joints. A bar and a jukebox that was playing the Cuban quarter tone stuff Ellen and I had loved in Havana.

And the Voice. Over the music the Voice. "Cannot understand, Mr. Andrews, in view of your other qualifications, why you made such ridiculous claims in the face of fact, because they would have been unnecessary. Your degree in rocket engineering, your responsible position. . ."

Every word I remembered, every word ran through my head in quarter tones to Cuban rhythms.

"Afraid I can't sell you any more, pal. Might cost me my license, pal. You're pretty drunk."

Not drunk enough, pal, not drunk enough.

Over street noises, the Voice. Over other voices, over the whirring whirling of the Earth in space, the Earth my spaceship carrying me even now through the void but to nowhere, until some day it would be my revolving coffin.

Snow and gay decorations and somebody saying Merry Christmas to you, my buying someone a drink, his buying back, his face coming suddenly into focus. Guy about fifty, with a beautiful-ugly face, broken nose, wide clear eyes, eyes that had seen the naked stars, the stars from space, steady and untwinkling. A spaceman.

He said, "You'd better straighten out, matey, before it gets you down for keeps. Anything I can do?"

"I'm not your matey. I'm not a spaceman."

195

"Don't gimme. You're Max Andrews."

"I'm Max No Difference," I said. "I'm a fake. I'm not anybody."

"Matey, I know you. You're the best mech in the game, and you're a spaceman." He leaned forward and his eyes, those wide clear eyes, got bright. "Listen, matey, things have looked lousy for a while, but they're looking up again. We're sending one farther out. To Jupiter."

"The hell we are," I said. "Listen, you got me mixed with somebody else. I never heard of a Max Andrews."

He said, "If you want it that way."

"It *is* that way."

§

I woke from the nightmare of the frozen instant again and sat up, struggling into awakeness to dispel the spell.

A hotel room again, but no purple flowers. A bigger room, a nicer room, with two beds. And my friend of last night, the spaceman whose name I didn't know, sleeping in the other bed. He'd brought me here to pull me out of it.

But not yet, not yet.

Necessity gave me the steadiness to dress very quietly, making not a single sound, so as not to waken him.

I didn't want to argue with him, because he was right. He was a good guy, this spaceman who knew me but whom I didn't know or didn't remember, and he'd brought me here to help me. He was right by his standards and his standards were right for him, but they weren't right for me because I was wrong. I was wrong and I wouldn't be right until this ran its course, if it ever did.

But how could I explain to him? How can you show someone else your nightmares?

I checked money in my wallet. Plenty of it. I must have wired back for some, got some somehow. I took out enough to pay for the room and left it on the dresser, and I got out of there quickly and quietly.

I needed a drink worse than I needed anything else, except maybe to die and get it over with, and my friend probably had a bottle there somewhere, knowing I'd need at least a pickup shot in the morning. But it was hidden and I didn't dare search for it. Spacemen, even ex-spacemen, are always light sleepers.

Eight o'clock in the morning, but I found a liquor store open.

§

Other bottles, other rooms. Day and night and crowds and solitude. Bars and drinks and a fight, blood on my face and on my knuckles.

Devils and a cold wind, and phantoms of the living and dead. Arguing with my father, with Bill, pleading with Ellen.

"Darling, darling, you understand, don't you? I've got to do this, I've got to let it run its course, I can't stop now.

197

Even if this is the big one, the last one, I've got to ride it through."

Ellen didn't argue about the drinking; she understood.

Sometimes in semi-sober moments I wondered whether she would have, really.

But the dead must understand everything if they understand anything at all.

§

And one night, one unexpected night, street noises again and cheerful voices, happy voices.

People laughing, people blowing horns, people celebrating.

Suddenly more noises, crescendo.

Sirens and whistles, bells ringing. Bells tolling.

Somebody yelling at me, and the words came through, *Happy New Year*.

The bells and the sirens and the whistles and the yelling and the crowds and a big clock beginning to toll *bong, bong, bong*.

Suddenly it came to me what this was. Not just another damn new year after another Christmas; it was more than that. It came to me through the noise, through the gently falling snow, this is the turn of the century and the turn of the millennium, Jesus God, this isn't just another year, this is the year two thousand, the year *two*

2000

2000

thousand! Something to celebrate, something really to celebrate! Yell Happy New Year, Happy New Millennium. A bar with people crowding up to it three and four deep. I tried to push my way in, couldn't. Drinks being passed back. Somebody had an extra one in his hand, looking around for someone he'd been with. He shrugged, handed me the drink. "Luck, Old-timer!"

Buying drinks for others, being bought drinks, caught in the frantic frenetic gaiety of a *fin de siècle,* the manic madness of a *fin de mille.* Back-slapped and slapping backs, shaking hands meaninglessly, in and out of focus. Then the crowd thinning, melting away, the last of us put out at closing hour, out into the night, now a windless night, cold, clear and still.

Staggering away somewhere, up streets and down streets, across turf in what seemed to be a park.

A bridge over a pool, over a still dark pool.

I staggered onto the bridge, stood looking down over the low railing into the black water, the water so still and so black that I could see the stars reflected in it, gently dancing, light-years below the still dark surface. Water in which life developed, the water wherein we were born and grew and whence we crawled out into air and onto land and looked up with animal eyes, seeing lights in the sky.

Now drunkenly watching lights in water, the reflected stars.

I was falling toward the sky, toward the stars.

§

The white room again, but this time not a nightmare, just a dream. Or was it even that? Someone was bending over me, someone with chestnut hair. But my eyes and my mind came in focus and it wasn't Ellen. It was a nurse, white-uniformed, with chestnut hair the shade of Ellen's, but not Ellen.

Her voice wasn't Ellen's voice and it wasn't speaking to me. "I believe he's conscious, Dr. Fell."

Dr. Fell; it rang a bell; I do not like you, Dr. Fell. How did that ancient rhyme go? *I do not like you, Dr. Fell. The reason why, I cannot tell. But this I know and know right well: I do not like you, Dr. Fell.*

The nurse had stepped back and I turned my head and could see him. A big man with iron gray hair and clear gray eyes, a face that, except for the broken nose, looked a lot like the face of the spaceman who'd taken me to the hotel.

"Up to talking?" he asked me. His voice was deep, resonant; the voice of a man you could have confidence in.

I said, "I think I like you, Dr. Fell."

He grinned at me. "All of my patients think of that damn rhyme, one way or the other. I should have changed my name." He said, over his shoulder, "You may go now, Miss Dean."

To me, "How are you feeling?"

"I don't know yet. Was anything wrong with me, outside of—?"

"Exposure, pneumonia, malnutrition, delirium tremens. That's about all. Do you remember what happened?"

"I remember falling into a pool. That's all. Did I get out by myself?"

"You crawled out, yes. It was only a foot deep. But you lay there near the edge, wet and freezing, for God knows how long before anybody found you. But I'll tell you one thing; if it had been even half an hour longer, you wouldn't be here. And another thing—one more drinking bout like that one will be your last, even if you don't fall into anything. Do you understand that?"

"Yes," I said.

"Luckily for you, you're not an alcoholic, so I don't have to warn you against doing normal, social drinking—after you're up to it again. But another extended drinking bout—"

I said, "I understand. How do you know I'm not an alcoholic?"

"From your brother and from a friend of yours, Mr. Klockerman. They've both been here. Your brother's still around; he'll be back during visiting hours this afternoon."

"You mean they both came all the way here from the coast? Or—wait, am I still in Washington?"

"This is Denver. You're at the Carey Memorial Hospital in Denver."

"How long have I been here? What's the date?"

"You've been here eleven days. You were brought in at five A. M. on New Year's day, and it's now January 11th, a Tuesday."

"What year?" I just wanted to hear him say it.

He looked at me strangely and then from the way he spoke, he must have got the idea.

"Two thousand," he said. "The year two thousand."

§

The new millennium, I thought, when I was alone again. The twenty-first century, in the third millennium.

The future. I'd always thought of two thousand as the future. When I was in my teens back in the nineteen fifties, it had been the unbelievably distant future, a date so far ahead that it didn't mean anything.

Here it was. Here it was and I was in it.

And here and now I had to make peace with myself if I was to keep on living in it. I had to make myself face the truth, and face it without concealment and without bitterness. With not too much bitterness, anyway.

I must recognize that I was getting old, too old ever to get out into space, not even to the planets, that I'd had my chance and missed when I was young, that I'd had a miraculous second chance—no matter how slim a chance—in my late fifties, and I'd missed that too. And I was practically sixty now, and there wouldn't be another chance. So what?

Lots of people are space-nutty all their lives and never even come close. They keep on living, don't they?

Accept that, I told myself, and you'll be all right from here on in. Nothing really bad can ever happen to you again, because you'll never come close again, to be disappointed. Nor will you ever love again, as you loved Ellen; if nothing so wonderful as her love can ever happen to you again, then neither can anything so terrible as her death.

Remember, never forget, that you've never left Earth and that you never will. Remember that, and it's a downhill coast.

You expected too much. More for yourself than one man has any right to hope for. And you expected mankind to accomplish more in your lifetime than you had any right to hope for.

He'll reach the stars, and in this millennium. Where was he at the start of the last millennium, the year *one* thousand? Fighting mistaken crusades with swords and spears and bows and arrows. And before the end of that millennium he'd left the Earth and reached the nearest planets.

And where will he be before the end of *this* millennium?

No, you won't see it. But you're *part* of it, as you're part of mankind, and you can help. For as long as you live, you can help push, since you can't ride. You can help push rockets and men toward the stars.

§

The chestnut-haired nurse brought my lunch and I found that I was pretty weak, but able to feed myself and to eat a little.

When she took the tray away I asked her when visiting hours were, wondering if I'd have time for a nap before Bill came. But there was only half an hour, so I didn't.

I thought about M'bassi instead. Chang M'bassi.

What if he and not I had the right idea? Well, it was possible. Nothing is impossible. Who, here and now, can define the limitations of the human mind, the things man may be able to do now or eventually with that wonderful and mysterious thing that is his mind?

Who, here and now, knows even the exact relationship between mind and matter? A man is a chunk of matter in which is imprisoned a mind, and when either dies—I think —the other dies with it. But the body can move the mind, and who am I to say that, now or eventually, the power of the mind cannot carry the body, and with the speed of thought.

If that's the right road, I thought, more power to M'bassi and may he be the one to find the road and take at least a step along it.

But it's not for me. I'd be kidding myself if I even tried it, and I've kidded myself enough. Rockets are my racket, and I'll stick to them. And settle for pushing them, improving them.

§

Bill said, "Hiya, Max. Glad to see you're back with us."

I shook hands with him and said, "All the way back, Bill." He'd know what I meant by that, and he'd know he could quit worrying about me, if he'd been worrying.

He pulled up a chair.

I said, "Let's get details over with first. How am I set for money? Who's paying for this?"

"You're all right. Klockerman's got your stuff—he's holding it for you—and he checked your bank book and says there's enough left to pay your full bill here and get you back again."

"Did he check with the bank to see whether—?"

"Sure. You'd wired them for money twice and they'd sent it, but that's figured in. Oh, by the time you get back to work you may owe one or the other of us a couple of hundred or so, but nothing enough to worry about."

"Good," I said. "Another thing. I talked to Fell, but forgot to ask him how much longer I'd have to stay here. Has he told you?"

"Checked with him on my way in just now. He says about ten more days and you'll be able to travel, but that you shouldn't go back to work for at least a month after that. Will you come and stay with us in Seattle? Merlene and the kids'll be crazy to have you, and so will I."

"I—do I have to decide that right now, Bill?"

"Of course not. I didn't mean to push you. And I ought to tell you you've got alternatives. Klocky, M'bassi and Rory have all put in bids for you. You've got some swell friends, Max."

"And swell relatives, Bill." I turned and looked at him

squarely. "Listen, Bill," I said. "In case I do decide to come to Seattle there's one thing I want to talk out with you first, and while we're alone."

"Shoot."

"It's about Billy. Do you mind if I—" I'd started to say, *if I try to give him the Dream,* but that wouldn't be Bill's language. "Do you mind if I talk space to him, try to make a starduster out of him?"

"Merlene and I have talked that over," he said quietly. "And the answer is no, we don't mind. It's up to Billy what he wants to do and be." He grinned suddenly. "Unless he changes when he grows up, he won't *need* any pushing from you. He's almost as bad as you used to be, Max."

"Good," I said. "In that case, Bill, I'll probably spend part of that month's rest-up with you. Not the first two weeks, probably, because I'll be—well, the second two weeks, when I'm stronger, will be better for me to be with the kids. They're pretty strenuous for an old man, when he's down."

"Great. I'll tell Merlene we'll have you the second two weeks. About the others, know yet who you want to spend time with first? I can let him know for you and save you writing."

"No, I haven't decided yet. But I'll appreciate it if you'll do this, Bill. Wire or phone all three of them that I'm out of it, and okay. All the way okay. Will you do that?"

"Sure."

"And keep a tab of how much the wires or calls cost. Also how much your trip here cost."

He laughed. "The calls, sure, but don't be silly about

the trip. A vacation from my family, and hell I've always wanted an excuse for a trip to Denver. Max, this used to be a *cow* town. About the biggest one, I think. And they've got museums of the Old West here, and I'll bet you can't guess where I've been staying."

"My God," I said, "don't tell me there are still such things as dude ranches?"

There were, and he was staying at one and having the time of his life. Probably almost sorry I'd recovered consciousness and coherence because now he'd have to grow up again and go home to his family.

My kid brother, riding a horse, playing cowboy, living in the past. My wonderful kid brother.

§

Letters came. One from Merlene saying how glad she and the kids would be to see me, that Billy especially was all excited because I was coming.

Letter from Bess Bursteder. *"I'm writing because Rory's awfully busy. He's changing jobs, Max. He's not been too happy at Treasure Island for quite a while now. He's been having trouble with the directors, doesn't see eye to eye with them on a lot of things. So he's taking another job and we're moving there this week end. It's still a head mech's job, but at a smaller rocket port and it won't pay quite so much. That doesn't matter, though, if he's happier in the work, and he will be, since they're giving him full authority over the mechanical end, no restrictions on whom he hires* and fires, nor on the time he allocates to each job—and that's the big beef he's had with the port directors here; they've been trying to get him to cut corners and save a few dollars.

"I know you'll be glad to know where we're going—because it's Seattle. Now and from now on you can kill two birds with one rocket blast in your visiting because we'll be living in the same city as your brother and his family. We hope to get to know them better, too. I liked your sister-in-law an awful lot the one time I met her. At the party in Los Angeles when we celebrated your getting your degree, remember?

"We're not buying a house there until we've had time to look around, but we both flew up there last week end and rented an apartment to live in meanwhile—and it's got a guest room for you. We're moving in Saturday and Sunday and we'll be settled down and ready for you by the time you get here. You are coming; don't give us any argument about that. Wait a minute; Rory's here looking over my shoulder and he says if I'm through he wants to add something. I'll turn it over to him. Bess signing off."

Rory's stubby handwriting took over. "Swell you're going to be with us, Max. Suppose you'll be going back to your old job at L. A. but if you don't want to, there'll be one for you in Seattle any time you want it. You just read what Bess wrote about the hiring and firing. Keep your chin up."

It put my chin up, to get a letter like that. And it decided me on Seattle.

Another letter the next day undecided me. It was from

M'bassi and it was a brief hurried scrawl. A paragraph telling me I should by all means come and stay with him while I was convalescing, and then:

"*Max, I think—I hope—that I'm on the verge of success. I want your help. Please come here.*"

That put a different look on things.

What did he mean, he was on the verge of success—that he could teleport himself, or that he thought he could do it soon?

And how the hell could *I* help?

Or, damn his wonderful black hide, was that just bait to get me there, by arousing my curiosity?

But Jesus, what *if*—?

It was hard to make up my mind, until two days later a letter came from Klocky.

"*Max,*" he said, "*I'm worried as hell about M'bassi. He's off on one of his mystical sprees. He's been fasting and taking drugs, and that's a hell of a dangerous combination. He's so thin he doesn't throw a shadow, and he won't listen to any common sense I try to talk to him. He can't go on like that much longer.*

"*If you feel up to it by the time you leave there—and I won't blame you if you don't—I think you ought to take him up on his invitation, just so you can be with him and try to get him straightened out. He's crazy to try whatever he's trying. If he doesn't starve himself to death he'll end up as a drug addict—no, I guess he has too much will power for that. But what he's doing is dangerous, just the same.*

"*God knows why, but you've got as much influence on*

211

him as anybody except Gautama Buddha, and I think he needs you.

"If you decide to stay with him, let me know when you're coming and I'll pick you up in my hellie so we can have a talk before I take you around."

That made up my mind for me, all right. It also got me out of the hospital three days short of the ten Dr. Fell had predicted. Maybe I did a little exaggerating to him about how well and strong I felt, but I got away with it.

§

Klocky looked just as he did the day I left him. I don't know why that surprised me, after only two months, but it did. Maybe because those two months had seemed like twice that many years.

He gripped my hand so hard it hurt. "Good you're back, Max. Missed you. Let's go to the coffee shop for a few minutes and talk before we go to my hellie."

I remembered Klocky never liked to talk while he piloted, or even while he drove a ground car. I nodded.

Over coffee, I asked him about M'bassi.

"Nothing new that I know of. Haven't seen him for two days—but listen, before we talk about M'bassi, let's talk about you a minute. You're coming back to your job with me, aren't you?"

"I—I don't know, Klocky. I don't think so."

"It's open. I marked you down for indefinite leave of absence. And I need you, Max."

I grinned at him. "That isn't what you said the day I left. But seriously, I want to mech a while again, I think. It's what I need—for a while anyway. Grease and oil and grit and soot on my hands. Physical work."

"Max, you're not getting any younger. You can't do mech work all your life."

"For another few years I can. After that—I'll see. But don't keep that job open for me, Klocky."

He shrugged. "It's your business. I'll keep it open for a while, though, in case you change your mind. And I'll give you a mech job meanwhile, but damn it—"

I shook my head. "Not at L. A., Klocky. It would be embarrassing for both of us to have your former assistant working as a grease monkey. I know where I'm going to work." I told him about Rory's change of jobs and his offer.

"Okay, if that's the way you want it." I could see that he was relieved that I didn't intend to mech at the L. A. port.

"Klocky," I said, "I haven't been reading the papers much. Has the appointment been announced?"

He knew what appointment I meant. He nodded. "Kreager, Charlie Kreager."

The name didn't register, but apparently Klocky knew who he was. "Good man?" I asked.

"Damn good."

That was what I wanted to hear and I let it go at that. How much Klocky knew or guessed of the details of what had actually happened, I didn't know, didn't want to ask. We let it go at that, but it knocked a worry out of my mind to know that a good man would be supervising the construction of the Jupiter rocket.

I said, "Now about M'bassi."

"On second thought, Max, there's nothing else I need to tell you. You'll know the score the minute you see him. Maybe better if I don't tell you any more than I have—not that there's much more to tell."

"We're wasting time then. Let's go there," I said.

§

No answer to our knock. A square pink corner sticking out from under the door. I pulled it out and opened the pink telegram envelope. It was the telegram I'd sent the day before telling M'bassi when I'd arrive. It must have been delivered twenty-four hours ago at least.

The door wasn't locked; we went in. Knowing, both of us, that we were too late, knowing what had happened.

Inside, the light layer of dust over the smooth surfaces.

The door to the little room, the room without furniture, the cell, was bolted on the inside. I knocked only once; then Klocky and I looked at one another and I nodded. He's fifty pounds heavier than I; he backed up and ran at it, throwing his shoulder against it. The bolt snapped.

M'bassi was smiling, lying there.

He lay on his back on a strip of canvas, wearing only a breechclout. His rib case looked like a bird cage. His eyes, wide open, stared fixedly through pinpoint pupils upward.

We made the routine checks before we made the routine phone calls. But we'd known, both of us, from the moment that our knock on the outer door hadn't been answered, that we were too late.

M'bassi wasn't there. His body was there, but M'bassi?

I wished that I could believe that M'bassi had gone *somewhere,* not just that M'bassi had gone.

§

I wish that I could believe not in mortality but in reincarnation or individual immortality; I wish that I could be living again in another body or, God help me, even watching from the edge of a fleecy cloud in Heaven or out through the dirty windowpane of a haunted house or through the dull eyes of a dung beetle or on *any* terms. On *any* terms I want to be watching, I want to be there, I want to be around, when we reach the stars, when we take over the universe and the universes, when we become the God in whom I do not believe as yet because I do not believe he exists as yet nor will exist until we become Him.

But I've been wrong so I can be wrong. *Make* me wrong, damn You, show me that I'm wrong, show me that M'bassi had cause to smile.

Show Yourself, God damn You, make me wrong.

2001

2001

"We'll see better from here, Billy," I said.

I'd parked the hellie behind the hill and we'd walked up it, one of the low hills that ringed the site. Five o'clock of a clear October evening, the sun getting low. Three hours before the take-off of the Jupiter rocket, but there were others there even before us, finding good spots on the best hills. By three minutes after eight, take-off time, these hills would be filled with people.

"You're sure, Uncle Max, that down by the fence—?"

"Not nearly as good, believe me." I grinned at the boy. "I know you want to get close, but don't worry; you'll be closer to rockets than you'd get to that one at the edge of the launching site."

Forty-three feet tall it stood, and beautiful. God, how beautiful. Sleek and slender, shiny and Oh God there aren't any words for a rocket, a new one-man rocket that's going where no rocket has been before, to another world, farther out. Nearer where we're going.

I saw the disappointment in Billy's freckled face. I said, "Okay, there's lots of time. Go down to the fence and look at it from there, but then come back. The take-off will look better from here."

I watched him run down the hill. Ten now, he was. God, how fast the four years had gone since I'd first heard of this rocket, since I'd first heard of Ellen Gallagher. God, how fast the years go when they near the end. Constant acceleration, like a falling object. Be with you soon, Ellen, I thought; whether it's a couple of years or thirty years, they'll go like a flash. The speed of light? It's nothing to the speed of time.

I spread the blanket and sat on it, watching the rocket, watching Billy. He stood now at the high steel-mesh fence, pushing his face against it to be as close as he could.

I saw myself at ten, although there weren't interplanetary rockets to look at then, back in nineteen fifty. But I'd have looked at one like that, had there been one to look at.

I looked at one now, and I wanted to cry because I wouldn't be on it when it went to Jupiter. But sixty-one is too old to cry. You're a big boy now, I told myself.

Sun going down. Son coming up; not my son, but the nearest I'd ever have to a son of my own, plodding up the hill toward me, his eyes filled with stardust. Sitting on the blanket beside me.

The lost, longing look in his eyes. The look of a spaceman Earth-bound. The caged look.

Dusk, and more people gathering. Silent, most of them. Most of us. Silent in wonder at the thing that was to happen.

Dusk and the bright floodlights down there, down where it was going to start to happen, down there where a man with a light in his eyes like the light in Billy's eyes was getting ready to leave Earth, to escape from this poor two-dimensional surface upon which we three-dimensional beings crawl.

Escape, God how we all need escape from this tiny here.

The need for it has motivated just about everything man has ever done in any direction other than that of the satisfaction of his physical appetites; it has led him along weird and wonderful pathways; it has led him into art and religion, asceticism and astrology, dancing and drinking, poetry and insanity. All of these have been escapes because he has known only recently the true direction of escape—*outward*, into infinity and eternity, away from this little flat if rounded surface we're born on and die on. This mote in the solar system, this atom in the galaxy.

I thought of the distant future and the things we'd have, and discounted my wildest guesses as inadequate. Immortality? Achieved in the nineteenth millennium X. R. and discarded in the twenty-third because it was no longer necessary. Reverse entropy to rewind the universe? Obsolete with the discovery of nolanism and the concurrent cognate in the quadrate decal. Sounds wild? How would the word *quantum* or the concept of a matter-energy transformation sound to a Neanderthaler? *We're* Neanderthalers, to our descendants of a hundred thousand years from now. You'll sell them short to make the wildest guess as to what they'll do and what they'll be.

The stars? Hell, yes. They'll have the stars.

§

Dark now. "What time is it, Uncle Max?" "Four minutes to go, Billy."

The floodlights go off. There is a breathless hush. Thousands of people and a breathless hush.

Oh God, Ellen, if you could be here with me, to watch our rocket take off. *Our* rocket. But more yours than mine. You died for it.

Here waiting in the breathless dark I feel humble before it and before you, before man and his future, before God if there is a God before mankind becomes one.

THE END